inside: Are you falling for your friend?

THERE'S NO WAY HE COULD BE JEALOUS. . . .

Tara tugged on Noah's arm. "Look! The fireworks are starting."

Noah nodded, pulling her close as a burst of color exploded in the sky. Then he glanced back at Meg. Jeff's arm was draped casually over her shoulder, and Meg's head was resting lightly on his chest.

"Guess the fireworks in the sky aren't the only ones taking place," Tara noted as Jeff bent down and gave Meg a kiss.

"Guess not." Noah wanted to block out the scene that was taking place across the fire. What did he care if Meg kissed some guy? "Maybe we should start our own right here."

"Sounds good to me," Tara purred.

Noah met her lips with his. But as they kissed he found himself staring over at Meg. He watched, trancelike, as she kissed Jeff, their faces glowing under the amber flames of the fire. He'd never thought of Meg kissing anyone—or realized how much it would bug him if she did.

Love Stories

Summer Love

WENDY LOGGIA

BANTAM BOOKS
NEW YORK · TORONTO · LONDON · SYDNEY · AUCKLAND

RL 6, age 12 and up

SUMMER LOVE
A Bantam Book / April 1999

Cover photography by Michael Segal.

All rights reserved.
Copyright © 1999 by 17th Street Productions,
a division of Daniel Weiss Associates, Inc.,
and Wendy S. Loggia.
Cover art copyright © 1999 by 17th Street Productions,
a division of Daniel Weiss Associates, Inc.

No part of this book may be reproduced or transmitted
in any form or by any means, electronic or mechanical,
including photocopying, recording, or by any information
storage and retrieval system, without permission in
writing from the publisher.
For information address: Bantam Books.

Produced by 17th Street Productions,
a division of Daniel Weiss Associates, Inc.
33 West 17th Street, New York, NY 10011.

If you purchased this book without a cover you should be aware
that this book is stolen property. It was reported as "unsold and
destroyed" to the publisher and neither the author nor the publisher has received any payment for this "stripped book."

ISBN: 0-553-49276-4

Published simultaneously in the United States and Canada

Bantam Books are published by Bantam Books, a division of Random
House, Inc. Its trademark, consisting of the words "Bantam Books" and
the portrayal of a rooster, is Registered in U.S. Patent and Trademark
Office and in other countries. Marca Registrada. Bantam Books, 1540
Broadway, New York, New York 10036.

PRINTED IN THE UNITED STATES OF AMERICA

OPM   0 9 8 7 6 5 4 3

To Mom and Dad

ONE

MAYBE IT WAS because he'd been trapped in the car for way too long with his mother and Sam, his lovable, slobbery golden retriever.

Maybe it was because he'd drunk two two-liter bottles of water and hadn't made one rest stop.

Or maybe it was that he was only minutes away from the Atlantic surf splashing between his toes, the hot June sun beating down on his head, and Meg, his best friend, whom he hadn't seen since last summer.

Whatever it was, when Noah Ridgley pulled the Jeep Grand Cherokee into the gravel driveway of his family's summer home, he practically bounced off the SUV's walls.

"Looks like the Williamses have already paid us a visit," his mom commented, smiling up at a hanging basket bursting with red geraniums that hung from the hook on the side porch. When she opened the car door, Sam bounded out and promptly began to befriend every bush in sight.

Noah raced up the sidewalk and jiggled the key in the lock. "Hel-lo, summer," he said, letting out a slow whistle as he opened the door and stepped inside, the scent of sand and ocean filling his nostrils.

Dropping his backpack and duffel on the cracked linoleum floor, he opened the white miniblinds and squinted in the bright sunlight that flooded the kitchen. Then, after taking a quick, perfunctory glance around the downstairs, he jogged up the center stairway to his room. The door was open, and except for the new navy bedspread and matching floor rug, things looked just as they had when he'd said good-bye the past August. He gave the mattress a good thump and yanked open the window before running back down. After a pit stop in the bathroom, he and his mom carried in bag after bag of summer supplies, beach chairs, and enough suitcases to dress a small army. "Now the fun begins," Mrs. Ridgley said, staring at the mountain of bags that filled the kitchen.

Noah rinsed off two glasses from one of the cupboards and poured them each a glass of water. "I don't suppose you'd let me out of here for a while?" he asked, putting on his most hangdog expression.

His mom glanced at her watch. "If you promise to go grocery shopping later, I guess I can do without you for a while." She ran her fingers through her short brown hair. "And after all that time in the car I definitely need to take a shower."

Gulping down the rest of his drink, Noah splashed some cold water from the kitchen faucet on his face and then pushed open the screen door.

"Give my best to Meg!" his mom called as the door banged behind him. "That is where you're headed, right?"

Noah grinned as he jogged around the corner. Did she have to ask?

Meg Williams was possibly the coolest person on the planet. And if anyone knew that, it was Noah. Because for every summer for the past eleven years, Noah had spent every single day with her.

The year before Noah had started kindergarten, his parents had decided to rent a beach house in Silver Sands, just slightly north of Virginia Beach. Back then his parents didn't have a lot of money, so instead of renting a place by themselves, they opted to share. The real estate office had paired the Ridgleys, from Roanoke, with the Williamses, from Philly. The Williamses had two daughters: Natalie, age eight, and Meg, age five—like Noah. The adults had hit it off immediately, and soon Meg and Noah were busy bugging Nat, building sand castles, and racing hermit crabs along the shore.

The two families had shared a summer house ever since, until a few years ago, when Brilliant Gold, the oceanfront place that sat adjacent to Avalon, the Ridgley/Williams house, was renovated and put on the market, only to be snapped up immediately by Meg's parents. Noah had been majorly bummed when the Williamses told his family they were going to move, but the idea soon grew on him. Not only would Meg be right next door, but they could hang out on Meg's spacious oceanfront deck instead of in his cramped backyard. Not to mention that with Meg and Natalie's old bedroom now vacant, he'd have a lot more room for his stuff.

Meg's pristine white house faced the water, and Noah's cedar-shingled home was situated directly behind it, his backyard abutting hers. His view wasn't as glamorous as Meg's—just a quiet, sleepy street—but from the second floor you could see a sliver of ocean if you craned your neck right.

"Why, Noah!" Mrs. Williams exclaimed when he rang their bell. Meg's mother looked as polished as ever in plaid Bermuda shorts and a sleeveless yellow sweater. She gave him a big hug and kiss, then laughed and wiped his cheek to get rid of the mauve lipstick she'd marked him with. "How are you?"

"Fine, thanks."

"And your parents?"

"They're good. My mom and I just got in. My dad's driving down on Friday."

"I'm afraid that Meg couldn't wait for you to get here before she started on her tan." Mrs. Williams shaded her pale green eyes and squinted down at the beach. "She's out there somewhere. Just follow the sounds of Stereohead, or whatever it is you kids are listening to these days."

Noah laughed. "Okay. See you later."

He was psyched. With a clear blue sky and a

sizzling sun, it was a perfect beach day. And he was on his way to see Meg. Summer had officially begun! As he walked across the boardwalk and down the rickety wooden steps, the salty taste of the ocean air met his lips, while above him a lone pelican soared on the soft summer breeze.

The residents of Silver Sands had a long stretch of shimmery beige sand to themselves. Noah loved Silver Sands more than anything. It was the kind of place families came back to year after year. Where shopkeepers remembered you.

Where I'll have the chance to do some serious hooking up, Noah thought excitedly, smiling at a group of girls sunbathing on a nearby beach blanket. Everywhere he looked these days, girls caught his eye. Tall ones. Short ones. Thin ones. Round ones.

Might as well just say every girl. It was easier. And true.

It took him only a few minutes to spot the Williamses' blue-and-white flowered umbrella, tilting back toward him in the bright sunlight. Slipping off his thongs, he jogged down the beach toward it, wincing as the hot sand burned his toes.

But he halted when he got near the umbrella. He'd made a mistake—this wasn't Meg's after all. A shiny new cooler sat propped up in the sand next to a sleek silver boom box, its antenna broken off at the tip, playing a familiar song Noah had heard that morning. Spread out underneath the umbrella was a giant blue beach towel splashed with bits of yellow.

But these were details, minor details, considering

5

the beautiful female specimen reclining at his feet.

Not to mention her tiny, pale blue crocheted bikini.

Now that was a major detail.

The girl's hair was long, and a golden, summery blond . . . the color Meg's turned only after they'd been at the beach for weeks. And her legs were long too; in fact, they were so long, Noah couldn't help but stare at them like a drunken sailor. The beach goddess lay with her face and neck under the umbrella's shade, her softly curved body glistening in the sun. All he could see of her face was a pair of ruby red lips, slick with gloss, and a tiny, strong chin.

Noah's heart began to pump. This girl was hot. And it was the beginning of the summer, too soon for any other guys to have hit on her yet. Maybe he would be the first. Taking a breath, he wiped his palms on his wrinkled, ketchup-stained shorts, cursing himself for ordering those extra french fries on the ride down. But who would've guessed he'd see a girl like this? He'd been expecting only—

The girl sat up and ripped off her sunglasses. "Noah!"

Noah staggered back in the sand. "*Meg?*"

She leaped up and flung her slender arms around his neck. "About time you got here. I've been bored out of my mind!"

Stupefied, Noah let himself be hugged. Then he yanked himself away and gaped at the blue-eyed blonde standing before him.

"Meg!" he repeated once he'd found his voice,

poking her bare shoulder accusingly. Now that he was only inches away, there was no doubt it was her. He hadn't spent eleven summers with her for nothing. But from far away . . . man!

"Who were you expecting?" she teased, hugging him again.

The smell of warm pineapple mixed with coconut oil tickled Noah's nose as he shooed away the little bikini strings that fluttered around her neck.

Speaking of necks, his had started to sweat. Had he actually been thinking of picking up *Meg?* His childhood pal? Meg was his buddy, for Pete's sake. Sure, he wanted to hook up . . . but not with her! He shuddered. What if he had used some cheesy opening line? The scene was too horrible to contemplate. *Not to mention the laugh Meg would have had at my expense!*

Noah stared at her. "You just looked different from a distance, that's all," he said. The slick residue of suntan lotion stuck to his hands, and he wiped them on his shorts. "Older."

"Older? Really?" Meg broke into a huge smile, then peered intently at Noah. "You look older too."

"I do?"

Meg reached over and squeezed his biceps. "A little taller, a little beefier."

Noah flexed his arm, proud that she'd noticed. "Well, I have been lifting for a couple of months."

Meg giggled. "I said a *little*. But it's true." She gave his cropped blond hair an affectionate tousle. "And your hair! It's so short!"

Noah reached over and mussed up her hair in turn. "Looks like someone's been hitting the Clairol."

Meg ducked away. "Only my hairdresser knows for sure." She dropped back down on her beach towel. "When did you get here?"

"About an hour ago," Noah said, sitting beside her.

"You can't believe the major ordeal we had on the way down," Meg began. "Not only was traffic bumper-to-bumper, but the geniuses who work on the roads decided that this was a perfect time to close one of the lanes. And then my mom got mad because I made her stop for a bathroom break." She popped open the cooler. "Anyway, who cares about all that? I'm just glad we're here."

Noah leaned back on his elbows. "Me too." He cracked open the soda can she handed him.

"Think you can handle tonight?" Meg asked, her blue eyes twinkling.

Noah tapped his stomach. "I'm always up to the challenge of a junk food bonanza."

Ever since they were little kids, their parents had allowed them to go crazy on their first night together, eating anything they wanted and staying out way too late.

Meg leaned into him. "I've got so much to tell you, I don't know where to begin," she said. "Can you believe we haven't seen each other in ten months? How are things in Roanoke? My schedule was killer this year, and everyone says junior year is going to be even—"

Just then two girls wearing bikinis and sun visors jogged by. One of them smiled over at Noah. He returned the smile, puffing out his chest ever so slightly.

"What's wrong?" Meg asked, breaking off.

Noah shook his head as slightly as he could. "Nothing."

Meg leaned closer. "Are you sure? You look all stiff. And what's with that silly grin?"

Noah let his chest and face muscles relax. "Didn't you see those girls?" he asked under his breath.

"What girls?" Meg asked, following his gaze down the beach.

His smile faded slightly. "The two girls giving me the eye," he prompted.

Meg got up on her knees and shielded her eyes from the sun. "Where?"

"Meg!" Noah pulled her back. "Way to be subtle."

Meg rolled her eyes. "Don't get your shorts in a bunch, Noah. No one saw me."

"Lucky for you."

"Yeah?"

"Yeah."

Without warning, Meg grabbed his hand. "It'd be even worse if they saw me whip your butt!" She arm-wrestled him onto the beach towel.

"You wish!" Noah cried. But Meg had taken him unawares, and within seconds she'd pinned his wrist to the ground.

Meg licked her finger and made an invisible mark in the air in front of him. "Williams, one. Ridgley, zero."

"Yeah, well, you took me by surprise," Noah grumbled, rolling away from her.

"Oh, don't go all sulky on me." Meg nudged his thigh with her toe. "I'm sure those girls were dying to meet you. Really." She paused. "That's why they ran in the opposite direction." She began to giggle.

Noah tried not to laugh—but one look from Meg and he couldn't help himself. "You think you're pretty funny, don't you?" he said with a grin.

"Think?" She giggled again, her long hair spilling over her shoulders, her eyes dancing. "I just forgot how much I love to bust on you."

"Yeah, yeah," Noah said. Meg could tease him about girls all she wanted, but the truth was that if any summer was going to be filled with hooking up, this one was it. After all, he was sixteen, he had his driver's license, and his body—specifically his chest—no longer resembled a carrot stick.

Noah gazed longingly at the sea of bikinis that paraded by. Then he looked thoughtfully at Meg, wondering how he could possibly have mistaken her for a hot new babe rather than his childhood best friend. She'd straightened out her beach towel and was humming along to the song on the radio.

He'd heard that excessive heat could warp your brain and make you think things you wouldn't normally think. *That must be what happened today when I first saw her,* he decided, flicking a drop of sweat off his forehead. In any case, Noah would be sure not to let that happen ever again.

Meg glanced at him. "If your wrist's sore from

that arm wrestling, dunking it in salt water would probably help," she said sweetly.

"I've got a better remedy." Noah bent over and scooped her up.

"Put me down!" Meg shrieked, swatting him.

"No can do," he said, hoisting her higher. "I forgot how much I love to bust on *you!*"

With smooth, even strides, Noah ran to the water with Meg in his arms, dodging beach umbrellas, coolers, and sprawled-out legs. The two of them fell in a heap in the surf, laughing and splashing.

"You'll pay for this," Meg sputtered, but her eyes were laughing.

Noah's eyes laughed back.

Summer—it was finally here!

Two

CUTE. QUAINT. FAMILY-ORIENTED. The adjectives describing Silver Sands' wholesomeness were endless. But sometimes you just had to cut loose. Live life on the wild side.

And that meant one thing: cruising the Atlantic Avenue strip in Virginia Beach, preferably on wheels, but on foot if need be. The main boulevard was lined with hotels, tourist shops, and restaurants, and filled with cars pulsating to blasting stereo speakers, carrying teenagers hanging their arms and legs and various other body parts out rolled-down windows.

Noah and Meg were in the thick of it all. They'd parked the car on one of the side streets and were weaving their way through the crowds that filled the boulevard. First-night tradition meant stopping by at least three fast-food places. Salads and fruit smoothies were forbidden. If it wasn't deep-fried or liable to cause tooth decay, forget it.

"Remember, you've gotta eat this fast or it'll blow away," Noah cautioned, pulling a hunk of sky blue cotton candy out of its plastic bag. He offered the bag to Meg.

"Don't worry," she said, ripping off a huge piece and stuffing it in her mouth. "It'll be gone in a minute."

Noah was having a great time walking and talking with Meg, filling her in on all that had happened since they'd last met. Noah loved that about their friendship. They could go ten months without seeing each other . . . but then they'd pick up right where they'd left off.

"By the time we get to Waves and Waffles, you'll be ready for more." He licked the sticky residue from his fingertips. "Unless you're too full." They'd already had fried oysters at Pete's and hot-fudge sundaes at Marnie's.

"And miss out on the greasiest, most cholesterol-filled fries this side of the beach?" Meg shook her head. "I don't think so."

Noah sidestepped a large man standing outside a shop, holding up a T-shirt that read Fall in Love . . . in Virginia Beach.

"It feels so great to be on our own," Noah said. He tossed the empty cotton-candy bag in a trash can.

"No being dropped off and picked up, no more nights trapped in the house," Meg agreed as they walked on.

"I wouldn't exactly say being back at the house is a bad thing," Noah said, a little hurt. That was one of the things he liked best about summer—spending nights lying around the house with Meg, watching TV and hanging out.

Meg put her hands up to his neck and massaged it. "I didn't mean it that way, silly. I just meant that it's nice to have the freedom to come and go as we please."

"That's better," Noah told her, mollified. They approached the grease-filmed take-out window of Waves and Waffles. "Hey, don't stop!" he protested as Meg quit rubbing.

Meg laughed. "How am I supposed to wolf down my fries if I'm busy giving you a massage?"

Noah shrugged. "You don't *have* to eat," he tried, scrunching up his neck and attempting to look as if he were in extreme pain.

"Tell you what," Meg answered. "I'll give you a rain check for tonight, if you promise to give me a massage later this week."

"Well . . ." Noah considered this.

"That means you're getting two massages and I'm getting only one," Meg pointed out.

"Okay. But I can't make any promises that it'll be good."

Meg took his hand, still slightly sticky from the cotton candy. "It's all in here." She tugged on one of Noah's fingers.

"Ow!" Noah yelped, yanking his fingers back. "They *are* attached, you know!"

"Oh, don't be such a baby," Meg said, interlocking her fingers with his and giving his hand an easy squeeze.

Noah squeezed back, hard.

"Ouch!" Meg cried, attempting to shake him loose.

"Oh, don't be such a baby," Noah said, smiling.

The sand was soft and cold, and the incoming breeze off the water made Noah shiver as he and Meg walked along the beach. If it weren't for the lights from the boardwalk and the hotels bathing parts of the beach in a pale glow, he wouldn't be able to see a thing. The crash of the waves sounded like thunder, and in the distance tiny lights blinked and flickered. Noah checked for discarded bottle caps or pieces of glass lying about, then sat down on a small sand dune.

Meg did the same, first unwrapping the sweatshirt she'd tied around her waist and pulling it over her head. "Chilly out here, huh?"

"Perfect sleeping weather." Noah took out a pink tablet from his pocket and picked off a piece of lint. "Tums?"

"Thanks." She popped it in her mouth and began to chew. A breeze picked up the long, silky hairs that framed her face, blowing them back. "Hey—did you hear that Marit Smith got her tongue pierced?"

Noah wasn't surprised. "You can always count on her for something radical."

Meg nodded. "That's definitely true."

"Have you run into Andy at all?" Noah asked. Andy Astley was a good friend of theirs who was working at a local bike rental stand that summer.

"Yep. He was giving some tourists a hard time for blowing a rim on a tandem."

"Is he still sporting that goofy haircut?"

Meg giggled. "He had a baseball cap on, so I'm afraid the answer might be yes."

Noah sighed. "The guy never learns."

"On the bright side, at least he *has* hair. You won't believe what those McNally brothers did. They're so obsessed with swimming that they shaved their heads to increase their speed. I haven't seen them, but that's what Daphne said."

Noah tried to imagine Brian and Scott McNally without any hair. It wasn't a pretty picture. "I'm sure they look ridiculous."

Meg wiggled her toes in the sand. "Hey!" she said, snapping her fingers. "You never told me how the prom went. You said in one of your rare E-mails that you finally got up the nerve to ask . . . what was her name? Madeline?"

"Madison." Noah winced as an image of Madison's tight black curls and even tighter black gown flashed into his head.

"So? How was it?"

"I try not to think about it."

"Why?"

The memory of that dismal night still depressed him. "Well, I thought going to the prom would be fun."

"Fun?" Meg tilted her head back and laughed. "That shows how much you know."

"Yeah, well, I know now. Not only did I pay an insane amount for dinner and monkey suit rental, the couple we shared the limo with were totally obnoxious."

Meg looked ready to be entertained. "How?"

"We had to drive around town for an hour just so people we didn't know could see us in the limo. Madison's friend Leslie sneaked in a flask of vodka, and she barfed before we even got to the prom."

"In the limo?"

Noah nodded.

Meg wrinkled her nose. "Ewww."

Noah nodded again. "And once we were there, Madison spent most of the night running in and out of the bathroom with her phony friends while me and the other guys stood around in our tuxes and wondered what we were there for."

"To pay for everything and look good," Meg said helpfully. She hesitated for a moment. "Why did you ask her?"

"You mean to the prom?"

"Mmm-hmmm."

That was a question Noah had asked himself many, many times. The simple answer was that a bunch of his friends were going, and Noah had thought it would be cool to go too. And even though he hadn't really *known* Madison, she was cute and seemed pretty friendly. She'd even hinted to him that she'd like to be his date. But it hadn't taken long for Noah to realize that he was basically just an escort—and a meal ticket.

Noah shrugged. "She was cute."

"Cute?" Meg stuck out her tongue. "But is she nice?"

"Nice? I guess so."

Meg tucked her chin behind her folded-up elbows and shot him a curious glance. "Did you . . . ?"

Noah looked at her, puzzled. "Did we what?"

Even though it was dark, Noah could see Meg's cheeks flush. "You know," she said.

"Jeez, Meg." He gave her a shove. "Talk about blunt!"

"What? What's the big deal about telling me? It's not like I don't know you're a—"

"All right, all right, it's no big deal," he cut in, surprised to feel his own cheeks flush. It wasn't as if Meg didn't already know everything there was to know about his so-called sex life. Still, he didn't need to hear her say the *v*-word aloud. Especially in reference to him.

"No. We most definitely didn't . . . you know," he continued, shaking his head. "Not even close. I'm, well—"

"Me too."

"Oh." Feeling an odd sense of relief that he and Meg were still of the same sexual status, Noah picked up a fistful of clumpy damp sand and let it run through his fingers. "I'm never going to another prom," he said vehemently. "One night of torture was enough."

"Not even next year?" Meg gasped, as if he'd just told her he was going to join the nearest

19

monastery. "But you'll be a senior—you have to!"

Noah reconsidered his statement. "Well, not unless I get someone cool and normal to go with me."

Meg tucked her arm in his and squeezed. "Listen, if you're in a prom jam, I'll make a personal trip down to be your date."

Noah smiled at her, touched that she would do something so thoughtful. "Would you really?"

Meg paused, taking her arm back. "As long as you promise not to puke on me in the limo."

"No, seriously. That's really sweet," Noah told her.

"Hey, you're my friend." Then she giggled. "Besides, I love a good excuse to go shopping."

"Gee, thanks." Noah laughed. "You know what? This is going to be an awesome summer."

"What makes you so sure?" she asked, picking at the tiny, frayed wristband she wore around her left wrist.

"A, I can drive, B, I've got a job, and C—"

"You've got me," Meg put in, smiling.

"Exactly," Noah finished.

They talked for another hour or so before Noah finally stood up, brushing the sand off his legs. "I guess we'd better head back," he said, extending his hand and pulling her up. He'd had plenty of energy before, but what with the drive and the beach and the three thousand calories he'd consumed, crashing on his bed was suddenly sounding real good.

Meg gave him a sleepy smile. "Yeah."

As they climbed up the wooden steps, Noah stopped to shake the sand from his shoes.

"Don't do that!" Meg squealed, reaching out to stop him. "You've got to leave some in your shoes."

Noah rolled his eyes. The local folklore was that if you left the beach with sand in your shoes, you'd be sure to return the following year.

"I don't want to get sand in the Jeep," he explained.

Meg gave him a stern look. "Now, what's more important: a clean car or you here next summer?"

Noah pretended to think about it. "Um . . ."

Meg socked him in the arm. "I'm serious!"

"I know. That's what's scaring me." But just to be on the safe side, he did as she asked.

The drive home was a short one, and before he knew it, they were at Meg's door.

"G'night." Noah gave Meg a half wave.

"'Night." Meg yawned, arching her back.

Noah didn't doubt that she was very tired, but that was a fake-out gesture if he'd ever seen one. Trying to look as casual as possible, he walked the few feet to the low fence that separated their yards, hopped over it, and trotted up the steps to his back porch.

Then he raced up the stairs, two at a time.

He didn't quite remember when it had started, but he and Meg had an unspoken contest that whenever they said good night they'd race to see who could get to their room quickest.

And I'm going to kick her butt this time, Noah thought, thundering down the hall to his room.

His hand swiped the light switch as he bent to look over at the Williamses' house.

Meg's heart-shaped face, illuminated by her bedroom lamp's soft glow, grinned back at him.

Noah swore happily under his breath. How had she gotten up there so fast? Giving her a final good-night wave, he pulled down the shade, kicked off his sandals, and padded down the hallway to the bathroom.

With life as crazy as it was, it was nice to know that summer would always stay the same in Silver Sands.

Just like his friendship with Meg.

THREE

MEG'S BEDROOM WINDOW stuck a little bit, probably because it hadn't been opened since the previous September. With effort, she yanked firmly on the white wooden frame.

"Unnhh!" The window flew up, and Meg fell back on her bed, panting. Then, dusting her hands off, she stood and lifted the screen, which was a lot easier to open. Propping her elbows on the windowsill, she stuck her head outside and took in the beautiful summer morning.

Of course, the view from her other window was amazing . . . the ocean foaming and frothing on the shore, early morning joggers out for a run, pelicans swooping down for a bite to eat. Sometimes she could even make out dolphins playing far out in the surf. But the view from this window wasn't bad either.

This was the window where she could spy on Noah.

She'd done a pretty good job of it so far this morning. He didn't have a clue she was watching.

For the past fifteen minutes Noah had been working like a man possessed. First he'd dislodged the stack of aluminum lawn chairs from their winter sanctuary and hauled them into the daylight. Next came the glass tabletop, followed by the heavy stack of padded seat cushions and the table umbrella, which was propped up in the far recess of the storage shed. Meg had to put her hand over her mouth to hold back the giggles when he accidentally conked himself on the head with the pole.

With a sigh, she tore herself away from the window and changed out of her pajamas and into her white bikini, pulling a pair of shorts and a T-shirt over it. As she dressed she thought about how Noah had gone ahead and broken one of the cardinal rules of boy/girl best friendship: He'd gotten extra funny. And extra sweet. And extra cute.

Okay, that was three rules. But who was counting?

Meg returned to the window, marveling at what a year could do. Noah was wearing a pair of jean shorts and a navy blue polo shirt, his hair sticking up all over his head. Somehow the past ten months had turned him into a Tommy Hilfiger model.

When she'd seen him on the beach, she had to admit that she'd been more than a little stunned. His torso had broadened, and his legs and arms were much more muscular than she'd remembered. And when she'd hugged him, she discovered he wore cologne now.

24

But still, this was just Noah. Noah, the guy who had taught her to ride a bike, who'd pulled the biggest sliver in the world out of her foot when she ignored the no-bare-feet rule on the boardwalk, who challenged her to a watermelon-seed-spitting contest every year. Her Noah.

She'd heard that excessive heat could warp your brain and make you think things you wouldn't normally think. That must have been what had happened the day before, when she'd felt attracted to him, she decided, rubbing the grooves that had formed in her skin from leaning on the ledge.

Now Noah was in the midst of brushing off the sticky cobwebs and other assorted junk that had accumulated on the chairs during the past year. He lined the chairs up on the small cement patio and rubbed his hands together, seemingly satisfied with his plan. Then he disappeared inside the shed and reappeared a few moments later, dragging a bright green hose behind him.

Meg rotated her neck in a slow circle, working out the kinks. She smiled as a little brown bird on the tree next to her window began to chirp at its mother, crying for its breakfast. "I'm hungry too, birdie," she said, imitating its squawking.

This was a bad thing to do. Because with her mouth wide open, she was the perfect mark for Noah's hose . . . and his evilly aimed spray of water.

There were only a few cars in the Fish Market's parking lot when Noah killed the Jeep's ignition and pulled into a spot in the back marked Employee Parking on Monday afternoon. The restaurant was located right in the heart of tourist central, on a small inlet that drifted away from the ocean, off a road the city had never bothered to pave.

Noah smoothed down the front of the khakis he'd been told to wear, checked his hair in the rearview mirror of a large van, and then walked up the ramp that led to the heavy wood-and-glass front doors. The Fish Market had always been one of Noah's favorite restaurants, and he'd been psyched when he'd called this past May about summer work and Bruce, the manager, had offered him a job on the spot.

A blast of air-conditioning greeted Noah as he entered the restaurant's empty front foyer. He picked up a plastic-wrapped peppermint from a bowl on the hostess's desk, unwrapped it, and placed it in his mouth.

Don't be nervous, he told himself sternly. *Think about something to make you relax.* The expression on Meg's face when he'd blasted her with water that morning immediately popped into his mind—that was enough to make anyone laugh and relax. He smiled and took a deep breath. If he felt nervous again, he'd just think of Meg. She wouldn't let him down.

"Do you know where Bruce is?" Noah asked a harried-looking guy hurrying by him, dressed in faded jeans and a polo shirt and carrying a card-board box filled with tomatoes.

The guy stopped. "You're looking at him. What can I do for you?"

Noah stood tall. "I'm Noah Ridgley. I'm sched-uled to start today."

The guy placed the box on the floor and gave Noah a quick handshake. "Follow me." He led Noah down the hallway and into a cramped office.

"Ridgley, Ridgley," he said, shuffling through a messy pile of papers on his desk. "Here we go." He pulled out the application Noah had sent in and looked it over. A clock in the shape of a largemouth bass ticked overhead. Noah silently prayed that his job hadn't been given to someone else. What if Bruce didn't remember that he'd promised Noah a job?

"I really appreciate your giving me this busboy position," Noah said, hoping to refresh Bruce's memory.

"Busboy?" Bruce tossed the application on the desk and threw him a waiter's apron. "I'm running real low on servers so far, and you've got that wholesome college student look our customers like. If you're good, you'll make triple the money you would as a busboy. Sound okay to you?"

"Sounds great!" He hadn't been at work two minutes and he was already getting a promotion!

Bruce picked up his phone and punched in a few numbers. "Hey, it's Bruce. . . . Yeah. Who's on now? . . . Yeah? She's early. Okay. She's perfect. Let her know I've got a trainee for her, will ya?" He clicked off. "Follow me," he said, motioning Noah out of the office.

They walked briskly back down the hallway and through the restaurant's main dining room. Servers were setting up for the evening dinner rush, and busboys were filling pitchers with water and ice. Noah tried to stay calm, but it was hard for him to hide his excitement. Being a server meant tip city!

At the far corner of the room was a large mahogany bar, in front of which was a line of tall wooden stools covered in blue leather. A sophisticated-looking girl with bobbed, glossy black hair and dark brown eyes sat on one of them, writing something on a piece of paper. She wore the standard uniform of white shirt and khaki pants, which fit her well. *Extremely* well.

"This is the guy I just called about," Bruce told her. "He'll be trailing you tonight."

Me? Trailing her? Noah thought excitedly. *Yes!* He was suddenly very glad that he'd taken that breath mint.

She smiled at him as she reached for his hand, her full red lips parting to reveal a row of brilliant white teeth. "Hi. I'm Tara. I was just sitting here going over tonight's specials."

Noah shook her hand, hoping his wasn't too clammy. "Noah." As he felt his muscles tense up, he focused his thoughts on an image of a soaking-wet Meg. *That's it,* he thought as the tension seeped away. *Keep cool.*

Bruce clapped him on the shoulder. "Okay, Tara, you know the deal. Noah, you're learning from a seasoned pro. Check in with me before you punch out and let me know how your first night here went." With a curt nod, he strode off toward the kitchen.

"You're in luck, Noah," Tara said, her full lips curving slightly. "Tonight we're doing everything two by two."

Usually when people tried to spring a new ark joke on Noah all he did was roll his eyes, but the way Tara said it, in a friendly, almost flirtatious way, made him laugh.

"You sure I'm not going to bug you, following you around all night like a lost puppy?" he asked, slightly dazzled by her smile.

She tapped him lightly on his forearm. "I don't think that's going to be a problem."

Noah was still reeling from the fact that Tara had touched him as she led the way across a small bridge with hemp rope railings into an empty dining room. "Okay. There are three basic shifts. The first wave are the senior citizens, who come in for our early bird specials." She pointed to a blue neon board. "The seniors can be ornery, but usually they're okay, and even though they're not the biggest tippers in the world, they're repeat customers and somebody's grandparents, so be nice."

Noah nodded, distracted by her big, dark eyes and thick, curled lashes. He wondered how old she was. She had to be at least eighteen.

"Around six, families start coming in," Tara told him.

Hmmm. Maybe nineteen.

"Give anyone under four feet tall a cup of crayons—we cover the tables with white paper, perfect for spilled drawn butter or drawings of pet hamsters."

Tara's hair moved in perfect sync when she turned her head . . . as did some of her other key body parts. Noah wondered if she had a boyfriend. Because if he had a shot with a college girl—man, that would be a fantasy come true!

"The last shift is pretty much families and couples, so just go with the flow." Tara touched his elbow and pointed to a booth. "Let's sit down and go over the menu. It's pretty basic, really."

Noah sat down next to her in the booth, flushing as his khaki-clad thigh brushed hers. Rather than move back, though, Tara leaned in closer. Noah's heart began to pound. First he'd gone from busboy to server in a matter of minutes, and now he was under the tutelage of one of the most gorgeous girls around.

This could be the start of a beautiful romance . . . or at least a hot summer fling.

"Okay. Now see these little metal cups?"

Noah nodded. For the past two hours Tara had given him a dizzying lesson in restaurant mechanics, dropping in the fact that she'd just completed her first year of college (she was eighteen, Noah had learned). Servers in crisp white shirts and colorful ties scurried about, a few of them taking a moment to give him a brief smile or a quick hello. But Noah was too taken with Tara to really notice anyone else.

"When you begin your shift, make sure you've got a trayful each of sour cream, tartar sauce, and cocktail sauce. This is part of your side work." Tara turned to wag a finger at Noah. "And keep the trays in the refrigerator until you need them. Bruce is a nut about stuff like that." They moved down to the garnish area. "This is where we keep parsley sprigs, lemon wedges, lettuce leaves, that sort of thing." She smiled. "You know, to make the food look more attractive."

"There's a lot of attractive stuff around here," Noah tried, hoping he wasn't being too forward. Tara was so friendly and open that any initial shyness had disappeared.

Tara gave him an appreciative glance, turbocharging his heart. "Now that you mention it, I'd have to agree with you."

That was it. Noah's heart was practically beating out of his chest. Oblivious, Tara pointed to a small walk-in refrigerator. "In there is where we keep all of the desserts: key lime pie, cheesecake, fruit tarts. Reddi Wip is stored on the top shelf. Fresh berries are kept in the Tupperware bins. There are also gallons of extra salad dressing and honey mayo, but leave that to the salad girls. They'll get you what you need."

Reaching over, she straightened Noah's tie and pulled on his white dress shirt. "Are you ready?"

He nodded, momentarily intoxicated by the whiff of honeysuckle that floated over him when she was near. "If we go over any more stuff, I'm bound to confuse flounder with salmon and create total chaos."

"Don't worry. You'll trail me for the first two hours and then, if you feel up to it, you'll go out on your own. There's nothing to stress about." She gave his cheek a light pinch, a gesture Noah wouldn't bestow on a girl unless he really knew her.

Or really liked her.

"And besides," she continued with a wink, "I'll be keeping an eye on your every move."

Noah grinned. He would definitely be returning the favor.

"Hi." Noah whipped out his order pad. "Are you ready to order?"

The dark-haired girl on his left glanced at her friend, a mousy-haired blonde, and nodded. "I'll have a Coke."

"Me too," said the blonde.

"Two Cokes," Noah said, scribbling that down. "Would you like to hear our dinner specials?"

"Are you one of them?" the dark-haired girl asked, her expression gleeful. Her friend giggled.

Noah leaned down so he was eye to eye with the two of them. "They didn't have enough bread crumbs to cover me," he answered flirtatiously.

As he headed back to the kitchen to place his order, he could barely keep the smile from his face. He'd never had so much attention from the opposite sex in his life!

"You're doing great," Tara said when they crossed paths an hour later. "Everyone out there seems to love you. I haven't seen one unhappy table yet."

Noah beamed. "I'm having a great time," he said, holding the kitchen door open for her. "Thanks for your help."

"Anytime." Tara made a sad face. "I was kind of hoping you'd screw up so I could be around you more."

Noah gulped. "You were?"

"Uh-huh."

Flustered, he let go of the door, which promptly swung shut, forcing him to jump back while Tara jumped inside. Through the round circle of glass he could see her laughing.

"Catch you later," she mouthed with her full lips.

"Okay," Noah mouthed back, hoping his lips weren't too trembly.

Definitely okay.

He was sweaty and smelly and tired, but as he got into the Jeep and started the engine at midnight, Noah was pumped. So pumped that he rolled down all of the windows, stuck in his old Verve CD, and blasted it as loud as he could without blowing out the speakers.

He'd been more than prepared to meet a hot girl. And now he had.

I can't wait to tell Meg about Tara, Noah thought excitedly as he cruised down the deserted boulevard. *She's gonna flip!*

FOUR

T HE SURF SOAKED his legs as Noah stood on the shore, mesmerized. There was Tara, waist deep in the ocean, radiant in a white tank suit. A silver zipper stretched all the way to her navel. "Hi, Noah," she purred, her full lips parting slightly. "Come on in. The water's fine."

Noah began splashing out to her, half running, half swimming. He was almost there when he realized he had on his jeans, but it didn't matter. Not when a girl like Tara wanted him.

A college girl . . .

"Don't keep me waiting, Noah," she said silkily. "I'm a big tipper."

Reaching her, he slipped his arms around her tiny waist, pulling her close. Her lips were only inches from his, and he could feel her heart pounding beneath him.

"I've waited a long time for this," Tara whispered.

Noah nodded as he moved his mouth toward hers. "Me too. A whole day."

And slowly, deliciously, saltily, they began to kiss . . . until something began to tickle his face. Something soft and wispy. Something annoying. Something—

"Whaaa—?" Noah peered up at the face looming over him. Long strands of blond hair dangled over his cheeks. He swatted them away.

"You missed it!" the face's voice cried. Then the person pounced on his bed, jiggling the mattress so hard that the springs creaked.

"Missed what?" Noah mumbled, pushing Meg away and hugging his lumpy pillow as Tara's body slowly dissolved from his mind.

"Just the world's most awesome sunrise, that's all," she chirped.

Noah buried his head deeper in a last-ditch effort to salvage his dream. Why did Meg have to sound so peppy? That sort of thing was illegal in the morning. He squinted over at the tiny plastic travel alarm clock on the nightstand. It was way too early.

"Are you crazy?" Noah muttered, rubbing his eyes. "This is summer *vacation*. We're supposed to be *sleeping in*. You know, stay out late, sleep in late, no clothes except bathing suits allowed, et cetera, et cetera. Ring a bell?"

Meg strode over to the window and gave the shade a firm tug, sending it snapping up and letting in a blinding ray of light. "Do the words *clam dig* mean anything to you?"

He opened one sleep-crusted eye. "Maybe."

She bounced back onto the bed. Noah groaned. "Listen, today's forecast is perfect: sunny, a light breeze, and low humidity. Plus low tide is in about an hour. Perfect clamming conditions!"

There was no use in fighting being awake any longer. Noah opened his eyes wider to see Meg smiling brightly at him. She was dressed in a pair of cutoff jeans, a navy-and-white-striped T-shirt, and holey old Keds, a faded fisherman's hat pulled low over her forehead. She looked pretty cute.

"Andy's going to meet us down on the beach," she added. Then she wrinkled her nose. "What's that smell?"

"Last night's special. Deep-fried haddock."

"Ooh, I forgot." Meg shot him an apologetic look. "Are you real tired?"

Tara's smile flashed into Noah's head, giving him a stronger jolt than a triple mocha espresso ever could. "Nah, not really. I'll tell you everything after we eat." He swung his legs over the edge of the bed. "Speaking of which, what's for breakfast?"

Meg dangled a bulging white paper sack in front of him. "Fresh from Posey's. And they're still warm."

Noah licked his lips. Posey's Bakery made terrific doughnuts. He reached for the bag, but to his annoyance, Meg yanked it back.

"Uh-uh," she said, sidestepping out of his grasp. "When you're showered and dressed, we'll talk."

Before Noah could protest, Meg scampered out of his room and down the stairs.

Did I just think she looked cute? Noah thought as he pulled off his T-shirt. *I definitely need more sleep.*

"Do we really need to go through this again?" Noah asked Meg a little later that morning.

Meg shook her head, her long ponytail flopping from side to side. "No, not if you'll finally agree that I'm right." She turned to Andy. "Aren't you going to put your two cents in?"

Andy Astley looked up from the ditch he was making with his foot, his wavy light brown hair still in a state of sleepy dishevelment. "I don't know anything 'bout technique," he said, giving them one of his trademark wide-lipped smiles. "I'm just here for the free baked clams you promised to give me later."

Noah let out an exasperated groan. "Meg. How many times do I have to tell you? Sighing the clams takes less energy and achieves a maximum number of them." He peered down at the sand's surface, hoping to see some of the little keyhole indentations that would give his argument the upper hand.

"And how many times do I have to tell you? Raking them is *fun*."

The three were a good mile down the beach, where the landscape of wide, flat stretches of sand expanded into a craggy maze of large, sharp-edged rocks covered with green sea slime. Small waves lapped the shore, each time depositing a few more droplets in the puddles that lay pooled behind the boulders.

Noah was about to counterattack when he stopped short. Why were they wasting all this time arguing about clamming when he had news to tell? "You guys haven't asked me how last night went," he said coyly, mentally reliving his interaction with Tara.

"How was last night?" Andy asked automatically.

"Was your new boss nice?" Meg piped in, swinging her gray metal clamming pail between them. In her free hand she held a small garden claw spotted with rust. With her floppy hat, she looked like a little kid ready to play.

Noah grinned. "He was okay. But other people made the night interesting. One person in particular."

"You bonded with the dishwasher so soon," Meg marveled sarcastically.

Andy sniffed the air. "Or maybe he had a run-in with a walking fish stick." He and Meg cracked up.

"Hey, if you guys want to be lame, go ahead," Noah said, unperturbed. "Because I've got more important things to think about . . . like how I'm going to spend the rest of my summer with the most incredible-looking girl in Virginia."

"You are?" Andy asked, sidestepping a jellyfish.

Meg frowned. "Hitting on customers isn't cool, Noah. Especially on your first night."

Noah rolled his eyes. "She's not a customer.

She's a fellow . . . server," he said, letting the last word roll off his tongue.

"Server!" Meg exclaimed. "Weren't you supposed to be toting dirty salad plates to the kitchen?"

Andy gave Meg a shove. "Who cares about the job classification? I want details on the babe!" He stomped on the sand with his feet. "I'm here two weeks, and what do I have to show for it? Nothing. One night on the job and you're already meeting women."

"It was like fate," Noah told them. "See, Tara—that's her name—worked at the Market last year as a server, and—"

"But you were supposed to be a busboy," Meg cut in, her brow puckered.

"I know!" Noah grinned. "That's what I mean about fate! Bruce—that's the manager—thought I'd be good as a server, so he promoted me on the spot."

"And that's fate?" Meg asked.

"No, fate is that Tara happened to be working the same shift as me, and that Bruce put us together as a team."

"What's she look like?" Andy asked.

Noah rubbed his hands together. "Dark hair, dark eyes, and a body that won't quit."

Meg scrunched her nose. "Quit what?"

Noah laughed. "Quit making me forget every single order I placed."

"She was that hot?" Andy said, a twinge of envy in his voice.

"Think of the hottest girl you know and add fifty more hot points."

Andy's eyes widened. "Hotter than that Brazilian girl with the thong we met last year?"

"Hotter."

Meg tapped her claw against her pail. "Uh, can we get back to business here? This is getting a little too in-depth for me."

"What about Valerie Orshan?" Andy pressed on, knowing that Noah drooled over the leggy supermodel. "She can't be hotter than her."

Noah thought for a moment. "Tara's body is different . . . more like an hourglass. Really tiny in the waist, and really full in, well, other areas."

Andy licked his lips. "Does she have a twin?" he asked hopefully.

Meg blew away a strand of hair that had fallen onto her face, which was slightly flushed. "Are we here to go clamming or to talk about bimbos with big breasts?"

"Who said anything about bimbos?" Noah asked.

"Who said anything about big breasts?" Andy wagged his eyebrows.

Meg folded her arms across her chest. "Okay. Time to redirect this conversation. How far out do you guys want to go?" She started toward the water.

"Wherever you think," Noah called, waving his small spade in the general vicinity. But his mind was still on Tara. Maybe he could ask her to go clamming sometime, although he couldn't quite imagine her liking it when her manicured nails filled up with sand and clam guts. She didn't seem like Meg that way.

Meg made her way out to the fringes of the incoming tide. "Is this all right?"

"Looks good," Andy said, kneeling down in the sand a few feet inland. He scanned for bubbles.

Noah crouched beside Meg as she began to pull her rake through the wet sand. "So, can you believe I met someone already?"

Meg poked around in the sand with her fingers. "I didn't even know you were looking." She picked up a scallop laced with ribbons of yellow and peach. "Isn't this pretty? That's what I love about coming down here so early. You can find the best shells." She dipped the shell in the water and then tucked it in her back pocket. "I'll put this in my collection."

Noah nodded halfheartedly. What was she babbling on about shells for? Hadn't she heard a word he'd just said?

He flung a tiny dead hermit crab in Andy's direction. "You didn't ask me how old Tara is, dude."

Andy let out a deep groan. "Don't even tell me you scored with an older girl."

"Okay, I won't. I'll tell Meg." He felt almost giddy. "She's eighteen!" he crowed.

"Eighteen?" Meg shrieked, dropping the clam she'd just unearthed. "That's too old!"

"No, it's not," Noah said defensively. "You're always saying I'm the most mature guy you know."

"You are the man!" Andy cried, coming over and giving him a low five. "Eighteen! Man!"

"So why is she interested in you?" Meg demanded, picking up the clam and throwing it in her pail.

"Well, gee, I guess the answer is that she somehow finds me attractive," Noah said, irritated that he'd have to explain something like this to Meg.

She picked at the sand clumped beneath her fingernails. "I'd wonder about someone two years older. It's kind of sick, if you ask me."

"Sick would be turning her down," Andy called over his shoulder as he headed back to his spot.

"You've got that right." Noah ran his fingers through the tiny lines Meg had raked. "Besides, she doesn't exactly know how old I am. We were too busy discussing, uh, other matters." He smiled, as if he had some big secret under wraps.

Meg let out a chuckle. "Trust me, Noah. As soon as she sees your driver's license, you're history."

"I don't think so," Noah said, annoyed at both the chuckle and the comment. "Trust me, Meg. The girl was into me. I was there. I should know."

"Did you ask her out yet?" Andy yelled.

"Not yet." Noah laughed. "She's got a set of—"

Meg stood up hastily, rivulets of water running down her legs. "Listen, I'm not finding anything here. I'm going to move."

Noah peered in her pail. "But Meg, you've got half a dozen—"

"They're dinky," she told him quickly, adjusting the brim of her hat. "You two stay here, okay? I'm just going to go down the beach a ways."

"But why—"

"Really." She held up her hand to silence him. "It's better if we spread out. We'll find more that way." Bending over to grab her rake and pail, she splashed through the surf and plopped down fifty yards in front of them.

Andy crawled over beside Noah and sat down. "I guess she takes her clams seriously."

"I guess," Noah said, disappointed as he watched Meg set up her gear. They never spread out when they went clamming—the fun part was always that they did it together.

He turned his attention back to Andy. "Anyway, as I was saying, Tara's got a set of lungs like you wouldn't believe. I didn't get the chance to ask her out because she was busy bawling out the cook for forgetting to put the scallops on the fisherman's platters." He shook his head, smiling. "But the girl digs me, Andy. This summer is going to rock!"

Andy clapped him on the back, leaving a wet, sandy handprint. "Let the dames begin!"

After some backslapping, arm punching, and other guy-bonding moves, Noah and Andy got serious. Soon Noah found a cluster of tiny air bubbles. Some fast and furious digging resulted in two measly clams. He tossed them behind him, safe from the incoming tide.

"Hey, Noah?" Andy said a couple of minutes later.

"Yeah?" Noah splashed some water on his neck. It was starting to get hot.

Andy looked disconcerted. "You don't think Meg's bugged about that stuff you were saying about Tara?"

Noah scratched his head. "Nah. Why would she be?"

A wave came up and tickled their toes. As it receded, a handful of tiny holes bubbled up. Andy began to scoop fast. "I don't know. Just seemed like she got this funny look on her face when you started talking about Tara."

"That's crazy," Noah said. "If anybody can read Meg, I can." He watched as she balanced on her hands and knees, methodically moving her rake from side to side. "She was all annoyed that she didn't have a pailful of clams yet. She was just being competitive."

Andy shrugged. "Yeah, I guess you're right."

Noah nodded. Meg was like that. She'd act all friendly and calm about things, but underneath that smooth blond facade was a vicious competitor. Noah had always liked that about her.

Andy was busy poking a jellyfish with a twig. "Would you come on?" Noah admonished after a few more minutes had passed. "We're going to be feasting on six clams at the rate we're going." He hunched over and began to dig at a cluster of foamy little bubbles.

His concentration was intense . . . making him the perfect target for the huge clamshell that whizzed through the air and clipped him on the side of his head.

Noah looked over at Meg. Her shoulders were

shaking with laughter. "Heads up!" she cried.

Noah shook his fist at her, then chucked the shell on the beach. "Make that seven clams."

Later that day Noah decided to take Sam for a walk. Or more accurately, Sam walked him, yanking on his leash so hard his breath came in raspy, throaty dog gasps. Once they got down to the water, Noah would take off his leash. Noah didn't quite trust him not to dart off in between the beach chairs and umbrellas. The previous year he'd taken someone's bologna sandwich between his teeth and just run with it.

Soft afternoon sun lazily flooded the beach with light, and the warm ocean breeze still lured latecomers down to the water. Noah took a deep breath, filling his lungs with the scent of coconut oil and salt. This was one of his favorite times to hit the beach.

He and Sam hadn't gone very far when he noticed a dark-haired girl walking a tiny white powder puff of a dog a hundred yards ahead along the shore. The girl turned her face toward the breeze, her glossy black bob whipping back in the wind.

Noah's heart started to thump. Could it be? "Tara!" he called, jogging up to her.

She turned around and stopped. "Hey, Noah! What's up?"

In her low-waisted jeans and neon yellow bikini top, which revealed a tiny butterfly tattoo on her shoulder, Tara looked even better than she had the day before. Her abs were flat as a board, and her chest . . . well, that wasn't so flat.

Noah pointed to Sam, who was in the midst of sizing up his smaller counterpart. "Doing the daily dog walk thing. This is Sam."

"Muffins," Tara said, gesturing to the small, fluffy dog. Around the animal's neck was a tiny jeweled collar.

"She's cute." *Just like her owner,* Noah thought, barely believing that he'd had the good fortune to run into her.

"Don't say it too loud. She already thinks she's the queen." Tara took off her sunglasses, her clear brown eyes focused squarely on him. "You live in the Sands?"

Noah nodded. "On Dolphin Drive. About a quarter mile back."

"I know where that is," Tara said. "My friends and I are renting a house over on Crescent."

He made a mental note to go over there on a bike ride with Meg as soon as possible.

Muffins began to growl as a wave had the nerve to wet her paws. Tara laughed. "She views the ocean as her enemy."

Noah laughed with her. "Well, Sam thinks this whole beach is his personal stomping ground."

Tara bent down and stroked Sam on the head. "He's a beautiful dog."

"Thanks." Suddenly his mouth went dry. Ever since the night before, he'd been trying to come up with a plan to ask Tara out. Now seemed as good a time as any. "Hey, I was wondering," Noah began, raking his fingers through his semibuzzed hair in an attempt to look casual, "if you're not doing anything tomorrow night, maybe we could, uh, do something."

Tara smiled up at him as Sam slobbered her arm with wet kisses. "Tomorrow isn't good—"

"Hey, no sweat," Noah said quickly, feeling his cheeks redden. "Don't—"

"But Thursday is," she finished.

Yes! The prickles of perspiration that dotted the nape of his neck began to slide down his back. "Yeah?" Noah asked, hoping that he'd heard her correctly.

Tara nodded. "Give me a call later." She reached into her back pocket. "No self-respecting waitress goes anywhere without a pen."

Noah broke into a huge smile—this was really happening! "And no self-respecting guy goes anywhere without a piece of paper." He fumbled in his shorts pocket, then sheepishly stuck out his empty hand. "Or a clean palm."

Tara touched his skin with her fingertips, sending shivers through his body. He watched, entranced, as she wrote her number in blue ink on his hand, underlining it with a flourish.

"I'd better go," she said, tucking the pen back in her pocket. "I'm meeting a friend down on the pier."

"Okay," Noah said. "I'll call you."

"Cool. Bye, then." Tara waved and headed back down the beach, Muffins yipping at her toes.

"Bye," Noah called, watching as her curvaceous form retreated. He'd done it! He'd asked Tara out . . . and she'd said yes! He gave the water a jubilant kick, sending Sam into crazy, happy spasms. Sam's eager eyes looked at Noah expectantly, waiting for him to join in a late afternoon romp in the ocean.

Normally he would have. But today Noah shook his head. "Sorry, boy."

No *way* was he going to risk getting his hand wet.

FIVE

A COOL EARLY evening breeze ruffled Noah's hair Tuesday night as he opened the Williamses' sliding screen door and stepped onto their deck, balancing a tray of condiments in his free hand. Meg followed behind with a pitcher of iced tea and a stack of plastic cups. A wrought-iron table big enough to seat eight people was on their right, the cushioned chairs pulled out and scattered around the extra-large deck that provided a spectacular view of the Atlantic. Mr. Williams was manning the grill while Mrs. Williams and Noah's mother bustled about setting the table and carrying out platters of food.

"My mom couldn't believe how many clams we found," Noah said as he deposited the tray on the table.

"Good thing, considering that my dad forgot to pick up the baby back ribs." Meg poured herself a glass of iced tea, frowning as some splashed on the table. "You know, I could've used your and Andy's help this afternoon. I must've cleaned a gazillion clams by myself."

"Sorry," he said, his thoughts drifting back to Tara's butterfly tattoo. If he'd been shucking clams, he'd never have run into her. "We'll, uh, make it up to you," he said absently.

"I won't hold my breath." She adjusted the strap of her tank top. "Why couldn't Andy eat with us tonight?"

"He left me a message saying he met some girl at the bike rental stand." Noah dipped his finger in Mrs. Williams's homemade pickle relish and leaned casually against the railing draped with semidry beach towels. "Guess who I ran into on the beach today?"

"Daphne?"

"Nope. Guess again."

Meg chewed a hangnail. "The McNally brothers."

Noah grinned. "Not even close."

"Well, who, then?"

"Tara!" Noah exclaimed. "She was walking her dog." He waited for Meg's reaction, but to his dismay, she didn't even look up.

"What kind of dog was it?" she asked, flicking a piece of dead skin onto the deck.

What kind was it? Who cares? Noah waved his hand dismissively. "Some little white thing. But that doesn't matter." He paused dramatically. "What does matter is that I asked her out . . . and she said yes!"

At least this got a reaction. "She did?" Meg said, surprised.

"Tomorrow night I'm gonna call her and we're gonna make plans." He showed Meg his palm. "Doesn't she have pretty handwriting?"

Meg barely glanced at it. "I guess." She took a tray of cheeseburgers from her mother. "Thanks, Mom."

Noah frowned, touching the place where Tara had written her number. He'd gone home and copied it down, but still, it was nice to have the original on hand, so to speak.

"I hope you two are hungry," Mrs. Williams said as she went back into the house for napkins. "Dad's made a ton of food, as usual."

"I don't know about you, but I'm starving," Noah said, helping himself to a burger.

Meg spooned some pasta salad on her plate. "I'm not that hungry."

"*You* aren't hungry? Since when isn't your stomach a bottomless pit?" He chuckled. "Remember when you and Andy entered that hot-dog-eating competition on the beach? Remember that, Mom?" he asked as his mother and Meg's parents joined them.

Mrs. Ridgley sighed as she looked at Meg. "How you put all that food into that little body, I'll never know."

Meg groaned. "Just the thought of doing that again makes me sick."

Noah's face fell. Meg's ten-dog attempt was the

stuff legends were made of. "You've gotta do it again this summer, Meg."

She took a bite of pasta. "Thanks, but no thanks. My dance aerobics instructor would kill me."

"You're taking dance aerobics?" Noah asked, surprised.

"Is something wrong with that?"

"No, of course not," Noah said, hastily backpedaling. It was just that Meg had always liked the same sports he did: swimming, basketball, football. But dance aerobics?

"It'll help me get in shape for pom-pom squad, cheerleading, and majorettes," Meg explained.

Noah dropped the potato chip he was holding. "You're joining—"

Meg giggled. "Just ripping on you."

"Phew." Noah smiled and slathered some butter on his corn on the cob. "Hey, Meg?" he asked, out of their parents' earshot. He'd decided to bring up something that had been in the back of his mind all day.

"Hmmm?"

"Andy said something really crazy this morning."

"What?"

Noah spun the ketchup bottle on its base, wondering exactly how to word this. "He thought you were getting annoyed when I was talking about Tara."

She put down her fork. "You've got to be kidding."

Noah laughed, relieved. Of course Andy was wrong. "I know. I told him he was losing it—like you would care if I was going out with someone." He took a big bite of his burger.

"You're not going *out* with her, though," Meg said. She arched her eyebrow. "Are you?"

Noah took another bite. "Who knows?" he said, poking a wayward slice of tomato back in. "If things go well tomorrow night . . ." He licked the mustard from his lips. "I can't wait for you to meet her."

"Me neither," Meg said wryly.

Noah looked up from his plate. "Hey, don't sound so enthused. You guys would get along great."

"Yeah, I could talk about prepping for the PSATs and she could tell me what it's like to vote." Meg rolled her eyes. "I mean, come on, Noah. What would I have in common with someone her age? It'd be like hanging out with my sister."

Noah stuck his finger in his mouth and swirled it around. "You know what happens to people with bad attitudes," he said, his eyes mischievous.

"Don't you even dare," Meg said, getting up from the table and backing slowly away.

Noah leaped up and chased her across the deck. "Wet willie time!" Catching her at the railing, he crammed his wet finger into Meg's ear.

"Quit it, Noah!" Meg exclaimed, trying to get away from him. But Noah held her tightly, wiggling his finger around. "Promise you'll be nice?"

She yanked away. "Don't do that again!" She grabbed one of the beach towels from the railing and frantically wiped her ear, as if Noah had just injected her with the Ebola virus. "I mean it, Noah."

"Hey, a little spit in your ear never bothered you before," he said, caught off guard by how agitated she was. Had she forgotten all the wet willies she'd given him over the past few years?

"Well, it bothers me now," Meg snapped. "We aren't ten, you know."

"Well, we're not eighteen either," Noah retorted.

"What's that supposed to mean?" She crossed her arms. "I suppose you'd never give *Tara* the privilege of your saliva in her ear."

Noah laughed. "That would depend on how I delivered it."

"Yuck." Meg made a face. "Please spare me."

For some reason Noah didn't know what to say to that. They stood there for a few moments in silence. The longer they stood, the more awkward Noah began to feel. So he did what he always did when he was at the ocean—he stared out at the water, glimmering under an evening sky awash in reds, oranges, and purples.

Then he gave Meg a sidelong glance to see if she'd cooled off. For once he couldn't read her— her face was tilted into the breeze, and the ends of her hair rose and fell with each gust.

I guess we're too old for wet willies, he reflected sadly. He glanced over at their parents, deep in a fascinating discussion about the rise of mortgage rates.

At least we're not that old, he thought.

"Want to get a movie?" he blurted out. That would lighten their moods—watching movies together was one of their favorite things.

Meg paused, then shrugged. "Sure."

Noah reached over and squeezed her shoulder. "You're not still mad, are you?"

"That depends on how dry your hands are."

He held them up for inspection.

Meg nodded. "You pass."

They walked back to the table and Meg finished her drink, slinging the leftover ice over the railing. "We're gonna go get something at Movie Madness," she called to her mom.

"Feel free to watch it in the den," Mrs. Williams offered. "If you get something good, maybe we'll come in and join you." She turned to Noah's mom, who nodded her agreement.

Noah and Meg exchanged uneasy glances.

"It's not that we don't love you guys—" Noah began.

"But I think we'll probably watch it in my room like we always do," Meg finished.

Mrs. Williams took a sip of coffee. "Okay. There's plenty of junk food in the kitchen, so help yourselves."

"After this chowfest?" Meg asked, opening the sliding doors.

Noah patted his stomach. "Don't turn up your nose at junk food. I might take her up on it."

The house felt still and silent as they walked down the hallway to the kitchen, where Meg picked up her white cardigan from the closet and Noah fetched the car keys from his mother's handbag.

"So what do you make of that?" Meg asked under her breath as they walked next door to get the Jeep.

Noah leaped up and dunked an imaginary basket in the net overhead. "Of what?"

Meg looked at him as if he had three heads. "Obviously they didn't want us to be in my bedroom together."

"What?" Noah exclaimed. He glanced over at Meg, waiting for the punch line. But to his surprise, he realized that she was serious. "That is the dumbest thing I've heard all week!"

Meg slipped on her sweater. "Yeah, well, I'm not arguing with you. I just got that feeling from them, that's all."

Noah shook his head. "Our parents know us better than that." *Jeez, putting a move on Meg would be like . . . like making a pass at Andy!*

"I guess so." Meg let out a short laugh. "But you couldn't really blame them for getting worked up, no matter how weird *we* know it is."

Noah unlocked the Jeep. "What do you mean?"

Meg slid into the passenger seat. "Well, it does seem normal for parents to want to keep their two teenagers out of a place that's filled with temptation, and on safe, neutral ground where they can keep an eye on things."

"I guess," Noah said, only half convinced. The fact that anybody, especially his family, could even think he was capable of trying something on Meg made him kind of nauseated. He glanced over at

58

her, her face soft in the moonlight. Of course she was pretty—but she was Meg!

Her blue eyes twinkled as Noah started the car. "Maybe we should give them something to worry about."

Noah laughed. "We could really get them going." Then he sighed. "But they wouldn't buy it for long. Even though they seem like it sometimes, they aren't idiots."

She settled back in her seat, resting her shoes on the dashboard. "You're right. There have got to be tons of other ways we can make them sweat."

He nodded as a feeling of warmth slithered through his veins. *Now, if I brought Tara home—that would be something for my parents to sweat about. . . .*

"I've seen that," Meg said, pointing to a box on the rack of new releases. "And that, and that, and that."

Noah scratched his head. "Maybe you should tell me what you haven't seen. That might be easier."

"Well . . ." Meg walked slowly down the drama aisle, stopping in front of a display of Oscar winners. "We could always go for something classic, like *From Here to Eternity.*"

Noah picked up a triple pack of cassettes. "Or *Gone with the Wind.* You always make us watch it at least once every summer. I love how Scarlett is so determined to save Tara." *Tara.* A light went on in his head. Maybe he should save watching *Gone with the Wind* for when he was with Tara. . . .

Meg took the cassettes out of his hand and placed them back on the shelf. "Not tonight."

"You're right. Let's save it." He tapped the video card against the wall. "How about something more like *Alien,* or—"

Meg snapped her fingers. "Now you're talking classic!" She found a copy on the sci-fi shelf. "We're lucky it's still here."

"Why, if it isn't Silver Sands' own Siskel and Ebert." A tall girl with silky red shoulder-length curls and freckled arms popped into view.

"Daph, hi!" Meg gave her a big hug, and Noah followed suit.

The redhead folded her arms across her chest. "Nice of you to call me, pal. I've been sitting around bored as anything."

From the sparkle in her brown eyes, Noah knew she was lying. Daphne Katz probably hadn't been bored more than twice in her whole life.

"How long can you stay this season?" Meg asked.

"Six weeks," Daphne said. "The good thing is that's two weeks longer than last year. The bad thing is that's two weeks longer than last year."

"That's what I like about you, Katz. You never make sense," Noah kidded.

Daphne shot him an admonishing look. "Excuse you, I make perfect sense. I plan on having an awesome time here, but I met this guy back home and

60

things may or may not be kind of serious. I'm not sure yet."

"Oh, wow," Meg said, a slight twinge of envy in her voice.

"Yeah, wow," Noah said, putting on a fake dreamy expression. Girls could be so sappy.

Daphne grimaced. "Don't worry, I'm no lovesick fool or anything." She peered at their video. "Ugh. I hate that movie. All that monster mucus spewing everywhere. Give me Tracy and Hepburn any day." Her eyes grew suspicious. "And hey, didn't you guys see that, like, four times last summer?"

"No," Meg and Noah said at the same exact time. Then they met each other's gaze and cracked up.

It was five.

When Meg had lived at Avalon, her room was a mirror image of Noah's. Same cotton bedspread, same pull shade, same worn plank floor. Her new room was completely girly: antique double bed laden with seashell-appliquéd pillows, matching white wicker armoire and nightstand, carefully stenciled room border of starfish, lavender rug. Noah wasn't sure that someone with XY chromosomes was even allowed in.

Strolling around the room, he picked up the copy of *The Age of Innocence* that sat on Meg's nightstand, tossing the paperback from hand to hand. "You call this summer beach reading?"

"Sure, why not?"

"You're a better person than I am." Noah barely cracked a book during the summer, unless you counted his Barron's college guide, which his mom had forced him to bring along. He liked reading enough, but not at the ocean. Not during vacation.

There were too many other things to distract him. *Like Tara and her butterfly tattoo,* he thought happily.

As Meg put the tape in the VCR, Noah flopped down on her bed, balancing a big ceramic bowl of popcorn against his hipbone.

"Take your shoes off!" Meg squealed, waving a frantic finger at Noah's sand-covered sandals. Obligingly he kicked the offenders onto the rug and leaned back, stuffing a pale pink pillow behind his neck.

"You were the one who said I should keep my shoes sandy," he reminded her.

"Yeah, but not when they're on my bed." She lay down next to him, their shoulders touching. Their hips and legs would have touched too, if not for the popcorn bowl in between.

"I just love this movie," Meg said, grabbing a handful of popcorn. "Even the sequels are good."

"And the effects are incredible, especially when you consider that this was done over twenty years ago." Noah guzzled some orange soda.

"Okay, shhh," Meg said as the movie's opening scene began.

They munched together in silence.

About halfway through the film Noah sneaked a

peek at Meg. He always got a kick out of watching her watch a movie—the way she alternately scrunched her face up in fear or closed her eyes when she knew a particularly slobbersome scene was coming. It was just so cute. *And right about now . . .*

"Ewww!" Like clockwork, Meg's eyes flew shut. "Tell me when it's over!"

Noah laughed. "Like you don't know." Now the mother alien was going after Sigourney, and the entire place was drenched in alien phlegm. After a few minutes Noah reached over and peeled one of Meg's fingers back. "Okay, you can look now."

"Thanks," she said, staring at the screen through her slender fingers.

The screen grew dark and the music got scarier. Noah both loved and hated this scene. The first time he'd seen the movie it had pretty much terrified him, and ever since then, even though he knew what was coming, his body would tense and stiffen.

He felt a pair of eyes on him. He darted his to Meg. "What?"

"Nothing," Meg whispered. "It's just, uh, I love this part," she said as the alien burst out and nearly scared Sigourney Weaver to death.

"Me too." Noah rested his head against hers.

"Maybe we can rent *Aliens* next week," Meg suggested.

"Okay," Noah said absently as a long blond tendril fell across his chest. He began to think about their earlier conversation outside the Jeep. It was just so ridiculous. Noah could maybe see where their mothers were coming from if Meg were some girl from Roanoke or somebody he'd just met. But Noah couldn't picture himself hanging out in the bedrooms of any of the girls he knew back home anyway. He didn't feel comfortable with them . . . at least not the kind of comfort he felt with Meg. Hanging out with her was cool. He could be himself.

To prove his point, he let out a loud, satisfying burp.

Meg fanned the air in front of her. "You are *so* gross."

Noah raised an eyebrow. "Since when did that kind of stuff gross you out?" Meg could out-burp him anytime.

"Since Trevor Steel belched in my ear during Spanish class every day for ten months." She crunched a piece of ice. "Trust me. There are traits far more appealing to girls than Olympic burping ability."

Noah thought for a moment. Maybe she had something there. He nibbled on an unpopped kernel. "Make sure you point stuff like that out to me," he said. "You know, so I don't make a pig of myself when I'm around any girls. Especially Tara."

He lay back, lacing his fingers underneath his head. He still hadn't figured out what they'd do on their date Thursday. Dinner? A movie? But even that wasn't so simple. What kind of food did Tara like? What kind of movies did she watch? There were so many things to think about . . . and so many opportunities for looking like a total dork.

"Noah?"

"What?"

"Let's have breakfast Friday at the Sea Oats. My treat."

The Sea Oats Café was a popular Silver Sands restaurant—and home of the strongest coffee on the boardwalk.

"Okay. Yum." He nuzzled his head against Meg again, his cheek resting on a pillow of blond hair.

If only things with Tara would turn out to be as smooth as his relationship with Meg.

Then everything would be perfect.

SIX

"THERE," NATALIE WILLIAMS said, giving her bag a last vigorous shake. A pair of bike shorts fell out and joined the various other size-six garments on her bed, along with two pairs of sandals, a blow dryer, and a small silver makeup case.

Meg moved aside as a Temple University sweatshirt fell on her lap. "Is it really necessary for you to dump everything on your bed?" Her older sister's method of unpacking drove her crazy.

"Yes. It is." Natalie put her hands on her hips. "And who asked you anyway?"

Without even realizing she was doing it, Meg began to refold a purple T-shirt. "Gee, Nat, it's nice to see you too." Meg said a silent prayer of thanks that her sister was gracing them with her presence for only a couple of days.

Natalie reached over and ruffled Meg's already disheveled hair. "Sorry. Mom just gave me a lecture

67

on how I'm probably letting the house go to pot while you're all here for the summer. She pretty much succeeded in getting me completely stressed out."

Meg knew their mom could be a pain in the butt. But then again, so could Natalie.

"How's Noah?" Natalie asked, tossing her underwear into an empty drawer. "You two still joined at the hip?"

Meg nodded, watching the ceiling fan revolve. "I guess," she said listlessly, remembering the look in his eyes when he brought up Tara.

Noah.

The fact that he had a girlfriend was killing her. Okay, maybe Tara wasn't his girlfriend yet. But she could be. Worse yet, Noah *wanted* her to be. Meg was sure of it. Hadn't he been talking about her twenty-four/seven? Then again, they'd always talked about anything and everything. So the fact that Noah was sharing every little, annoying, heart-hurting detail shouldn't have come as a surprise.

But it sure made having feelings for him a whole lot harder.

"You guys have been friends for over ten years now, huh?" Natalie commented, running a brush through her hair.

"Yep," Meg agreed. Friends.

She sighed heavily. Natalie could be a witch on wheels, but Meg knew that her older sister could dish some pretty good advice if she had to. Part of Meg wanted to confide in her, to tell her that she'd been thinking about Noah a lot. . . .

"Do you remember when Noah talked you into getting your body buried in sand up to your neck?" Natalie giggled. "You looked so funny!"

"That was a hoot," Meg said dryly.

"Or how about when you two had the brilliant idea of sticking peanut M&M's up your nose and Dad had to pull them out with the tweezers?"

"Those were the days." Meg lay down on her back, thoroughly dejected. Of course Noah would never see her as a girlfriend. How could he? They were pals, buddies. That was all. "Enough about Noah, Nat," she said, swallowing back the lump that had formed in her throat.

Unfortunately, her sister was on a roll. "But he's always been there for you, hasn't he?" Natalie grew thoughtful. "I can still see his face when he ran up to the house, screaming that you'd fallen off your bike and hurt your arm. I think he was more upset than you were."

Meg nodded, remembering. When she was ten she'd taken a bad spill about a block from their house. Noah had wiped her tears and given her the melting Snickers bar he had in his bike basket before running to get help. And when her mother had taken her to the emergency room, Noah had insisted on coming and sitting in the muggy waiting area while the doctor took X rays and placed her fractured arm in a splint.

Noah's friendship had meant a lot to her over the years. Maybe even more than she'd ever realized.

I should be happy he met Tara, Meg thought, trying to convince herself that this was within the realm of possibility. *And even if things don't work out for them, how could I jeopardize years of friendship for what's probably just a silly little summer crush? Besides, it's not even like a real crush . . . it's not like I'm sitting around waiting for the phone to ring, or getting all mushy-eyed whenever Noah's around.*

That was it. She had decided—she wouldn't say a word to anyone. What would be the point? Noah had already met someone who apparently found him funny and cute and charming.

The bad thing was, her name wasn't Meg.

And the really bad thing was, Noah didn't care.

"What do you say we hit the beach for a while? Check out the guys?" Natalie asked, showing an uncharacteristic touch of sisterly bonding.

"I can't," Meg said reluctantly. "I promised Noah I'd, uh, help him out with something." She'd planned to stay far, far away from Noah that night. After all, watching him get dressed to go out with another girl wasn't exactly high on her list of fun things to do this summer. But when he'd called, begging for her advice, she'd weakened.

Buckle down, she commanded herself. *You can do this. You have to.*

It was better to keep things strictly platonic. Having her wisdom teeth pulled the year before had been painful enough.

Open-heart surgery could kill her.

★   ★   ★

"Ooh, looks like Hurricane Tara swept through here," Meg commented.

Noah leaped across a disorganized pile of T-shirts and dragged a wide-eyed Meg into his room. "Thank God you're here!" he cried.

"Hey, I like that," Meg said, circumventing a black blazer. "I think you should say that every time I come over."

Noah began pacing back and forth amid the rubble. "This isn't fun-and-games time here, Meg." His eyes flew to the clock. "I've got thirty minutes to whip myself into shape. Thirty minutes!"

When Meg didn't say anything, he shook her frantically by the shoulders. "Don't just sit there— do something!"

Noah was pretty sure he'd never been so nervous—not even when he'd had to read his paper about sexually transmitted diseases in front of his mostly female health class. He flipped haphazardly through his closet, tossing one pair of pants after another on the bed. Then he began to add polos and knit shirts to the pile. He even threw in a few tank tops for added color.

"Don't go postal on me, Noah. I'm giving up an afternoon at the beach for you." She bent down and sifted through the pile of shirts. "What about this one?" she asked, holding up an olive green polo.

Noah shook his head. "I need to be really tan before I wear that."

"Okay." She pulled out a rumpled white and blue cotton short-sleeved shirt. "How about this?"

He chewed his lip. "That's a good one, but I had it on the day I ran into her on the beach."

Meg let out a sigh. "I doubt she'd remember."

Noah couldn't believe his ears. "Are you kidding me? If I make a bad impression when I pick her up, she'll never go out with me again." He rummaged through a stack of shorts. "I don't want to look like some loser who has only one outfit. She's used to older guys with big wardrobes."

"How about these?" Meg suggested, holding up a faded pair of jeans.

Noah studied them. They'd looked good on him the other day—at least the bikini-clad girls in the Miata convertible on Fiesta Boulevard had thought so.

"Okay," he said quickly, yanking them out of her hands. Then he scowled and threw them on the floor. "I can't wear jeans," he muttered. "What if Tara wants to go someplace fancy?"

"That soft blue shirt that brings out your eyes and your dark khakis with the brown leather belt would be perfect," Meg proposed, unearthing said items.

"You think Tara will like it?" Noah asked, holding the shirt up to his face.

Meg paused before pulling her lips together and nodding. "Yeah. Yeah, I'm pretty sure she will."

"Thank you so much," Noah said, bending down to hug her, burying his face in the familiar scent of her hair. "You're the best."

She squeezed him back, then pulled away.

"Have fun, okay?" she said, turning to leave. "See you tomorrow morning."

"Yeah," Noah said, distracted as he thumbed through his too-empty wallet. He didn't want to think about the next day just yet . . . there were too many exciting possibilities to think about tonight.

"So where are we going?" Tara asked, smoothing down her skirt.

Noah loved what she was wearing: a long, butt-hugging black skirt and a short, midriff-baring top, accentuating her body in all the right places. "I thought I'd take you to Picante's," he said as he pulled onto the highway, hoping to strike the right mix of confidence and spontaneity. "It's Mexican. Is that okay?" If it wasn't, he'd made a list of five other appropriately cool places they could go.

Tara licked her lips. "I *live* for chicken quesadillas."

"They're awesome there," Noah said, relieved. "And Meg says the salsa is the best she's ever had."

"Who's Meg?" Tara asked, her brown eyes drifting over him.

Somebody call a lifeguard . . . because I'm in danger of drowning in Tara's long-lashed pools! Noah knew his thoughts were cheesy, but so what? She was gorgeous!

"Noah?" Tara prompted, startling him.

"Oh, uh, Meg's, uh, a good friend of mine. She lives next door."

Tara shook her head in amazement. "I could never be just friends with a guy."

"Why not?"

"There'd always be this underlying sexual tension between us."

"I know what you're saying, but it's different for Meg and me." Noah changed lanes. "We've been friends since we were kids. I never even think of her as a girl. She's just . . . Meg."

Tara checked her lipstick in the mirror. "That's sweet." She flipped the mirror back. "So, what are we doing after dinner?"

After dinner? He hadn't thought that far. Wasn't dinner enough? "I, um, thought I'd leave that up to you," he said, thinking fast. The fifty bucks he'd brought now seemed woefully inadequate. Of course a girl like Tara would expect more than tacos and hot sauce on a date. What had he been thinking?

"Well . . . are you into music?" Tara asked.

Noah opened up the glove compartment, where he'd crammed about ten CDs—jazz, R&B, even one of his mom's Yanni disks. "Totally. Is there something you wanted to listen to?"

"Not right now." Tara pulled a tiny rhinestone barrette from her purse and clipped back a small section of hair. "Have you ever gone to Blue Baja?"

The name sounded vaguely familiar. "No . . . what is it?"

"A really cool nightclub. And on Thursdays it's eighteen to twenty." She reached over and squeezed his arm. "Let's go there later. You'll love it!"

"Okay, sure," Noah said slowly, wondering if they'd pass by any fake-ID places along the way. "Eighteen to twenty, huh?"

"Yeah. It used to be sixteen to twenty, but that was like junior high, you know?"

"Right," Noah said, forcing himself to laugh. His mind reeled back to Meg's words on the beach. *As soon as she sees your driver's license, you're history.*

He smiled over at Tara as his hands clenched the steering wheel in a death grip. Meg was right. *If Tara finds out I'm still in high school, I'm toast!*

"Would you look at that line!" Tara exclaimed as they pulled up to the nightclub and parked the car. At least twenty people stood in line under a blue neon sign at the club's entrance.

Noah's palms began to sweat. How was he going to get out of this? *Tell her you don't have ID. Tell her you lost your wallet.* But that wouldn't work, he realized, wiping his hands on his khakis. She'd just seen him pay for dinner. What would Meg do in a situation like this? Noah frowned. She hated nightclubs. She'd never be in a situation like this.

Maybe I can bribe the doorman, Noah thought, feeling like throwing up as they walked toward the building. *Just when things were going so well . . .*

"Ooh! Michael!" Tara jumped up and waved excitedly to the bouncer. "I know him," she told Noah. "Come on." She pulled him up to the front.

A large guy with muscles the size of Noah's head and three gold hoops in his ear leaned over and gave Tara a kiss on the cheek. "Hey, Tara, whassup?"

"Nothing much." She smiled at him as he stamped her hand. "This is Noah, a friend of mine from work."

Michael nodded and stamped his hand as well. Noah stared down at the small blue smiley face. *I'm in,* he realized, his shoulders practically sagging from relief. *I'm not going to get carded!*

"Thanks a lot, Michael," Tara said.

"Anytime. Tell Carrie I said hi."

"Sure."

Yes! Noah thought excitedly. Then, swallowing back his nerves, Noah reached over and took Tara's hand. She laced her fingers in his as they walked into the club.

Music pounded from giant speakers perched in the rafters, and the acrid smell of clove cigarettes wafted through the air. People were packed on the dance floor that sat off to the right, while on the left there were clusters of bar stools and small, intimate booths. There was a stage at the rear of the club, where a band was really jamming.

"Where do we pay?" Noah asked, taking in the graffiti-littered walls, glittery palm trees, and neon flamingos that framed the interior archway.

Tara laughed. "We don't. That's one of the perks of knowing the guy at the door." She snaked her arm around his waist. "Are you ready to party?"

Noah had never been more ready in his life.

"You bet!" He gestured to the crowded dance floor. "Want to dance?"

"Sure!"

They squeezed their way in, rubbing shoulders with other sweaty club-goers. Finding a spot next to a large video screen, they began to dance.

As Noah suspected, Tara was a great dancer. She had this way of shaking her hair and swaying her hips at the same time that made his knees feel weak.

"This place is great!" Noah yelled over a particularly long guitar riff as he moved to the music. He bumped his hips against Tara's by accident. "Oops! Sorry."

Tara bumped into him on purpose. "I'm not."

After an hour of bumping and grinding, Noah was ready for a break. Not only did his feet hurt, but he was beginning to drip with sweat—and he was eager to talk to Tara, something that was virtually impossible on the dance floor. The music was too loud for conversation, and to Noah's dismay, Tara's style of dancing apparently wasn't limited to one partner.

First she'd been totally into him, dancing so close their bodies practically touched. But then, as she got into it, she moved away and swiveled from side to side, dancing with anyone within range.

Any guy, that is.

But every time he was on the verge of getting upset, she'd turn around and give him a wink or blow him a kiss, and he'd feel silly for reacting that way.

"I can't believe how many people I know here tonight!" she called over to him at one point, just after hugging a Will Smith look-alike dressed in a tight white T-shirt.

"Yeah, there seem to be a lot," Noah agreed dolefully. "So, do you want to take a break?"

"Oh, but I love this song!" Tara squealed as the band burst into a cover of a hit from the previous summer.

Noah remembered how he and Meg had made fun of the song. She'd never let him live it down if she saw him dancing to it.

But hey, if Tara liked it, he liked it.

"Ooh, baby, I'm lookin' for a good time," Tara sang along with the lead singer.

After they'd repeated the same verse about eighty times, Tara took Noah's hand. "I don't know about you, but I'm dying for a soda!"

Finally! Noah thought in relief. They made their way off the dance floor and to a just-vacated round table for two adjacent to the bar. Noah got two Cokes and a pile of napkins to soak up the sweat on his forehead, then joined Tara at the table.

"Are you having fun?" Tara asked, taking a gulp of her drink.

"Definitely," Noah said. A beefy guy wearing a shirt that said Eat This knocked him hard in the back as he passed. "The dancing's kind of wild out there, huh?"

"That's why I love it. It's like one giant dance party!"

Noah smiled—Tara's enthusiasm was contagious. And as they continued to talk, Noah found himself getting even more attracted to Tara, if that was possible. She had the prettiest face, and she had this habit of touching his skin lightly with her fingertips, sending little shivers of excitement up his spine. They didn't have too much in common—Tara was really into her sorority, she didn't like sports, and they had completely different tastes in music. But didn't they say opposites attract?

Suddenly Tara let out a gasp. "Look who's here! Luke!"

"Luke?" Noah repeated.

Tara put down her drink and whipped out her compact. "Luke," she said, styling her hair with her fingers. "The lifeguard who patrols the beach in front of the Fish Market."

Noah vaguely remembered a tan guy with a long blond ponytail.

Tara jumped up from her seat. "I've got to go say hello. I'll be right back."

"Do you want me to come with you?" Noah asked, not happy in the least to be stranded.

Tara shook her head. "Of course I would, but we'd lose the table."

"Oh . . . right." Noah shrugged, feeling helpless to do anything else. "Okay. I'll stay here."

"You're so sweet." She smiled, placing one hand on each of Noah's knees. "I'm really glad we did this," she said softly, moving in closer. "I normally don't go out with guys I work with, but there was just something about you. . . ."

Having her mouth so close tickled his neck, and his heart gurgled in his chest. *What are you waiting for, Ridgley?* Noah thought. *Go for it!*

Tilting forward, Noah kissed her. From the look she gave him when they pulled apart a few minutes later, he guessed he'd done okay.

"You taste like chicken quesadillas," Tara murmured, looking at him with her big brown eyes.

Just what every guy wants to hear. He winced. "Sorry."

Tara leaned in once again, her lips barely a centimeter away from his. "You forget. I live for chicken quesadillas."

SEVEN

WHEN THE PHONE rang at 9:00 A.M. on Friday, Noah smushed his face deeper into his pillow. *Meg has got to get a grip on this early morning thing,* he thought grumpily, letting the answering machine pick up.

"Hi, we're probably at the beach. Leave your name and number at the beep!"

She'd better have a good excuse for this.

When Tara's low voice spoke instead, Noah practically fell out of bed.

"Hi, this message is for Noah. Noah, it's Tara."

Noah kicked back his twisted sheets with a vengeance and ran down the hallway to his parents' bedroom.

". . . and I just wanted . . ."

He slammed his ankle against the doorway. "Damn!" he yelled, limping toward his mother's nightstand.

". . . to tell you that I had a . . ."

Noah yanked up the phone. "Hello? Tara?" The answering machine beeped. "Hold on a sec." He turned the machine off. "Hi!"

"Did I wake you?" she asked. "You sound out of breath."

Thank goodness she couldn't hear his heartbeat, which had sped up tenfold the moment he'd heard her voice. "No, not at all. I was just, uh, doing a few sets of push-ups."

"So that's how you get those muscles."

Noah laughed, flattered. After all, Tara was used to guys who were two years ahead of him in the workout department. So if she thought he was buff . . .

"I had a great time last night," Tara said.

"Me too," Noah said, pumping his fist. A girl calling a guy practically screamed *I like you*—not to mention that it was a definite turn-on.

"So listen," Tara went on. "I went in early to pick up my check and saw the schedule. We're both free tomorrow."

"We should definitely do something, then," Noah said, psyched that she'd been thinking about him.

"What about Busch Gardens?"

"Cool!" Sure, he'd been planning on going to the popular theme park later in the summer with Meg, but she wouldn't care. It wasn't like they hadn't been there a zillion times together already.

"What time can you pick me up?" Tara asked.

Noah hesitated. His mother probably wouldn't let him have the Jeep for the entire day. Then he remembered that his dad was driving down that afternoon, so his mother wouldn't be stranded after all. "Is eight okay?" he said, omitting the fact that he still needed to get his mom's permission.

"Perfect!"

When Noah hung up, he had a satisfied grin on his face. "A date at eight," he said happily, padding back down the hall to his room.

The house was eerily quiet, so Noah flipped on the old TV that sat on top of his bookcase for some background noise. There wasn't much on: Jerry Springer. Rosie O'Donnell. Lucy and Ethel. Tweety and Sylvester. Noah turned the TV off and stumbled down the hall to the bathroom, where his reflection made him groan.

After going through his morning routine, Noah shuffled to the kitchen, where his mom had left him a note on the table. She'd gone to the pharmacy with Mrs. Williams, and then she was off to pick up the charcoal grill they rented for the summer. *Walk Sam!* she'd added with a double underline. Sam was conked out in front of the refrigerator, his big chest lifting and falling with each heavy breath. Nudging him gently aside with his toe, Noah opened the door and peered inside.

Nothing particularly appealed to him. *I could always run out and get something,* he thought. Maybe Meg would be up for it.

Meg! He was supposed to meet her at the Sea

Oats Café! He checked the clock. *I'm only thirty minutes late,* he thought, deciding that wasn't too bad. *And once she hears why, of course she'll understand!* he realized, suddenly anxious to share his great Tara news.

Images of pancakes oozing with blueberries and warm pitchers of maple syrup floated before his eyes as he ran upstairs and pulled on a pair of orange-and-blue swim trunks and a light blue T-shirt. Stuffing his wallet in the tiny zippered pocket, he shook Sam awake, clipped on his leash, and took him for a few quick laps around the house.

When he got off his bike at the outdoor café that overlooked the boardwalk ten minutes later, he was surprised to see the waiter clearing a plate from Meg's table. A half-drunk glass of orange juice and an empty coffee cup sat in front of her. A deep lavender sun visor shaded her face, and her hair was in two braided pigtails.

"Hi!" Noah said, sliding into the empty plastic chair across from her. She'd snagged a primo location, right on the boardwalk. "You already ate?"

Meg just looked at him. "Well, seeing as how I've been waiting for you for over half an hour, I decided to do something crazy—I ordered breakfast."

"I know I'm really late, and I'm really sorry. But I have a good excuse." He signaled the waitress. "A large grapefruit juice and a stack of blueberry pancakes."

Meg raised an eyebrow. "I'm waiting."

"I was on the phone with Tara," Noah explained

excitedly. "It was so sweet—she called to tell me what a good time she had last night."

"The khakis must've worked," Meg remarked.

"And how!" Noah reached over and patted her hand. "Thanks for the fashion advice. I couldn't have gotten dressed without you."

"Hey, I couldn't let you go out wearing plaid and stripes or something," Meg joked. "Who knows what you would've done in that crazed state you were in?"

Noah nodded. "And you were right. I was stressing out so bad, and we ended up having the perfect date. First we went to Picante's, where we had the most awesome nachos—"

"You went to Picante's?" Meg interrupted, her voice surprised.

"I know I said that I was thinking of Italian, but suddenly, when we were in the car, I got this craving for Mexican . . . and you and I always have a great time there, so I thought, why not?"

She circled the rim of her near-empty glass with her finger. "Oh. Well, um, did she like it?"

Noah leaned back as the waitress put his juice on his paper place mat. "She's already dying to go back." He snapped his fingers. "Maybe the three of us can go there sometime!"

"Maybe."

"I can't wait for you to meet her. She's awesome." He sighed, remembering how great she'd looked on the dance floor. "And after dinner, we went to Blue Baja."

Meg crinkled her nose. "That disco over on Florham Boulevard? But you hate that kind of music!"

"It's really more of a club than a disco," Noah said. Then he laughed. "To tell you the truth, I was barely even listening to the music."

"Don't they card people?"

Noah grinned. "Another perk of dating an older woman: Tara knew the bouncer. We breezed right in!"

The waitress brought over his pancakes, and Noah practically inhaled them, he was so hungry. "Want some?" he asked Meg, waving a fork-stabbed, syrup-drenched piece of pancake in her direction.

"No, thanks."

Noah shoveled in another bite, loving the feel of the warm sun on his arms.

"Well, I'm glad you had fun," Meg said, rearranging the jelly packets in their plastic holder.

"Wait," Noah said between chews. "I've been saving the best part for last."

"There's more?"

He grinned. "We made out in the car for fifteen minutes! She has these amazing fingernails, and she does this little tickle thing—"

Meg covered her ears. "Ewww, Noah. I don't need to know that."

Noah glowed. "While you and Daphne were fighting over the remote control, yours truly was playing tongue hockey with a college sophomore."

"That's fine if you just want to fool around, but what about commitment?" she asked. "Do you really think that an eighteen-year-old girl is going to be interested in something permanent with you?"

Commitment? Who said anything about that? Noah shrugged. "We're not talking marriage license here, Meg. We had fun. No strings attached." Of course, he wasn't *opposed* to a long-term relationship . . . but he also wasn't opposed to a good old-fashioned summer fling. "She's an amazing kisser," he added, his lips going soft at the memory.

"Ridgley! Williams!" Noah looked up as Andy and two other guys they hung out with, Travis and Jeremy, screeched to a halt on their mountain bikes next to their table.

"Hey," Noah said, giving them each a loose handshake. "What's up?"

"This is perfect," Andy declared, flipping up the rim of his baseball cap. "We're on our way over to the courts at Brookside for a pickup game of hoops. We were just saying we needed to get some more guys to play."

Travis brushed his floppy blond bangs out of his thin, angular face. "Yeah, with you two we'll only need to find one more dude for a little three-on-three action."

Noah downed the rest of his juice. "Sounds good. Let me just pay my check and we're out of here."

Jeremy balanced his bike on one wheel. "How do you want to set up the teams?"

"Let's say the three of you against Meg and me and whoever else we find," Noah suggested.

Meg cleared her throat. "Uh, guys? I can't do it. I'm going to the beach with Daphne."

Noah tossed a handful of bills on the table. "Beach, schmeach. You can do that any day." He got up and stretched his legs. "Nobody's stolen the nets yet, huh?" For some reason, someone thought it was fun to take the nets from the hoops every year.

"I'm serious, Noah," Meg said as they stepped outside the restaurant. She tugged down the hems of her gray spandex shorts. "I told Daphne I'd go with her to get a pedicure at Beauties by the Bay, and then we're going to spend the day down at the beach." She paused. "You guys are welcome to join us."

A pedicure? Instead of basketball? What had gotten into her? Noah chewed on his lower lip. "Meg, we need you. You're an awesome shooter."

"Yeah," Travis echoed, rolling back and forth on his bike. "If you don't play, we're gonna have to find two more dudes."

Meg shrugged. "Sorry. Like I said, I already made plans. Looks like you're on your own."

Andy let out a disappointed sigh. "Okay, guys. Let's hit it."

Noah stood stubbornly rooted in place. He couldn't believe Meg was passing up a chance to shoot hoops to work on her tan!

"I don't understand why you're acting this way," he said in a low voice as the guys started pedaling off.

"What way?" She tilted her visor back, the sun shining on her cheeks.

"Like . . . like a girl!" he exclaimed. "I mean, since when did you care about pedicures?"

Meg put her hands on her hips. "I know it's hard for you to believe, Noah, but I *am* a girl."

"Yo, Ridgley! The courts are gonna be filled if you don't hurry up!" Jeremy yelled.

Noah shook his head in dismay. "Duh, Meg, I know you're a girl. But it's not like you act like one or anything."

"And what's that supposed to mean?" Meg asked, her eyes narrowing into thin blue slits.

Noah sighed. "Look, I don't want to fight with you. Go have fun with Daphne, all right? I'll catch you later down on the beach."

"Don't do us any favors." Turning on her heel, she jogged down the boardwalk.

Guess she got up on the wrong side of the bed, Noah thought as he got on his bike and caught up to his friends. *Well, thanks to my wake-up call, at least I got up on the right one.*

The air was only slightly cooler down by the ocean than it had been on the sticky blacktop of the basketball courts. Even the incoming breeze was heavy and warm.

Noah plodded through the sand carrying his

knapsack and an extra towel. The beach was pretty crowded this afternoon, and it took him a full five minutes to spot Meg's umbrella.

"*Hola,*" he said, tossing his stuff down next to Daphne, Meg, and Kelsey, who lived in the house next to Daphne. They were sprawled out on their stomachs on a faded patchwork quilt. Magazines and empty Snapple bottles lay scattered around them.

"Hi, Noah," Daphne and Kelsey said in unison, propping themselves up on their elbows. Meg lay with her face pressed against the quilt. She lifted her hand in what Noah guessed was a wave, although it might have been some sort of involuntary spasm, given the lack of enthusiasm she showed.

Great, he thought. *She's still mad.*

"You guys must be about baked by now," he said, spreading out his towel and dropping down beside Meg.

Daphne tossed him a plastic tube of SPF 30. "I swear by this stuff."

"We missed you," Noah said to Meg as he pulled off his sweaty T-shirt and slathered some lotion on his damp chest. "We ended up playing with these three local guys who thought they were the next Chicago Bulls."

"Well, I didn't miss you," Meg said, her voice muffled.

Noah poked her ribs through her purple suit. "Are you still mad?"

Meg turned her head to Daphne. "Am I still a girl?"

Daphne nodded solemnly. "I'm afraid so."

She buried her face once more. "Then yep, I'm still mad."

Noah reached in his knapsack and pulled out a vinyl-lined cooler bag. "I brought some Bomb Pops from the freezer," he said temptingly, handing one to Daphne and one to Kelsey. "But I only give these to people who are nice to me."

Meg bolted up and ripped the last ice pop from his hands. "Then arrest me." She balled up the paper wrapper and tossed it at him.

He lay back beside her as Daphne and Kelsey began a discussion comparing the merits of Speedos versus swim trunks.

"Don't be mad," he said, nudging her shoulder. "I'm not mad at you."

Meg squinted up at him. "Why would you be? I haven't done anything wrong."

"Well, what have I done?" Noah asked, bewildered. Meg was almost never crabby like this. "If you're still sore that I was late this morning—"

Meg shook her head. "It's not that."

"Then what?"

She took a deep breath. "This morning, at the Sea Oats. You just expected me to shoot hoops with you guys."

Right. I met her for breakfast and asked her to hang out and play. So the problem would be . . . ? "I'm missing something here, Meg. You like shooting hoops."

She sighed. "Yeah, but not all the time. I don't always want to do guy stuff."

"Guy stuff? Since when is shooting hoops guy stuff?" He leaned over and took a bite of her ice pop. "Sounds a little sexist if you ask me, Williams."

"Would you ask Tara to shoot hoops with you?"

"Tara?" He broke out laughing. "Of course not!"

"Why not?" Meg asked.

"I don't even know if she can play!"

Meg shook her head. "Yeah, but that's not why you wouldn't ask her."

"Yeah, it is," Noah argued. "And besides, she's not the type. She's not like you." It was awesome to watch Meg on the court, her blond hair flying and her long legs a blur as she leaped in the air and swished the ball through the net. But Tara? He could picture her doing lots of things, but playing Michael Jordan wasn't one of them.

"What's that supposed to mean?" Meg asked, tossing the Bomb Pop stick aside.

Noah blinked back at her—her eyes were angry and her body was tense. He didn't understand what he'd done wrong. And suddenly he didn't want to deal with this anymore. He stood up and chucked his wallet on the blanket. "She doesn't make stuff all complicated," he said, sounding more agitated than he meant to. "I'm gonna go cool off. Literally."

The ocean felt like melted ice on his skin as Noah jogged out through the foamy surf and dove into an incoming wave. He let the water massage his game-weary muscles for a good fifteen minutes before diving back under and swimming to shore.

As he cut through the waves, he realized he'd forgotten to tell Meg about his upcoming date with Tara.

But why bother? he thought. *In the mood she's in, she'll only give you grief about that too.*

No, he'd keep every delicious detail to himself. Or at least most of them, because Noah was counting on having some that would be too good not to share.

EIGHT

A T EIGHT O'CLOCK sharp on Saturday morning, Noah picked up Tara at her house and
headed for Busch Gardens in Williamsburg. He'd
been hoping for some sort of crucial moment in
which he'd be able to display his stellar critical
thinking skills and NASCAR driving techniques,
but unfortunately, the drive was completely un-
eventful.

After Noah coughed up the park admission fees
for the two of them, they picked up a map of attrac-
tions and walked hand in hand down a hill and into
the heart of the picturesque park, with its theme of
seventeenth-century European villages.

"Didn't you just love that?" Noah asked a little
while later, after they scrambled off a roller coaster
billed as the world's tallest and fastest.

Tara shrugged. In her shorts and cleavage-
friendly top, she was easily the sexiest girl he'd ever

gone out with. "It was fun, but there's one at Six Flags that's even better."

"Are you kidding? This is our favorite!"

"*Our* favorite?"

"Meg's and mine," Noah explained. "We went on it five times one day last summer." He smiled at the memory. They'd ridden with their arms up the entire ride.

"That's nice," Tara said, linking her arm in his and giving him a squeeze. She came to an abrupt stop in front of a cart filled with trinkets. "Oh, look . . ."

This was only their second official date, but Noah had learned one thing fast: Tara was the biggest shopping enthusiast he'd ever met.

It would be the same thing every time. Noah would say, "We've got to go on this," as he studied the map for the next attraction. Then Tara would stab the map with her shiny red fingernail. "And look, it's right near some gift shops! You won't mind if I just peeked in, would you?"

"No, of course not." Then, before he knew what had hit him, they'd spent an hour traipsing in and out of countless European-themed gift boutiques, where Noah had felt compelled to pay for, among other things, the T-shirt, key chain, and hand-painted Venetian mask Tara had so desperately wanted.

As they made their way into the next "country," where a fresh new supply of shops threatened both Noah's patience and his wallet, he decided to take matters into his own hands.

"Want to take a break from the shops and go on a few rides first?" he suggested hopefully.

"All right," Tara said, sounding surprised. "I'm sorry. Have I been boring you?" Her brown eyes stared into his, turning his brain to mush.

"N-Not at all," Noah stammered. He couldn't help but notice all the appreciative stares Tara was receiving as they made their way through the park. "I could never be bored with you."

Tara slipped her arm around his waist, her hand resting slightly below. "You're one of the sweetest guys I've ever met, Noah."

Her touch—and her placement of it—made Noah almost swallow his gum.

"How about the race cars?" he asked quickly when he saw Tara's eyes flitting over the list of area gift shops. He pointed to the racetrack that was now in front of them. A couple hundred people stood snaked in line. "The line isn't that bad."

Brightly colored antique-style race cars chugged along a cement track complete with safety straps to ensure that the cars stayed on course. No wild curves. No unexpected twisting and jerking. No added expense.

No reason not to do it.

"If you'd like to, sure," she said. She pulled him along beside her. "As long as I can drive the car," she warned, rising up on her sneaker-clad toes.

"I wouldn't have it any other way," Noah said with a grin.

★   ★   ★

The kid behind them was getting exasperated. "Just step on the gas pedal, lady!"

"We don't need any help from the peanut gallery," Noah called over his shoulder as Tara yanked on the steering wheel. He glanced nervously at her. Her mouth was set in an angry line, and her arms were stiff with tension. "We must have a defective car or something."

"You're holding everybody up!" The kid began to beep his horn.

"This happened to Meg and me on the bumper cars down on the beach," Noah told her. "We got stuck in this corner with this big group of middle-schoolers, and Meg had to—"

"I could do without the trip down memory lane, Noah," Tara snapped, thumping the side of the car with her hand. "Can't you do something?"

So Tara wasn't exactly happy. "Isn't there some sort of height restriction on this?" he joked, extending his leg over to her side and pumping the gas pedal.

With a lurch, the car shot ahead, sending their heads snapping forward.

"Ow!" Tara's hand flew to her neck. "You could've told me you were going to do that."

Noah sighed. "Sorry."

Maybe shopping would be easier after all.

"Phew, it's hot out here." Tara fanned herself with her park map. "So what kind of show is this?" Her bangs had started to wilt and her shorts had gotten pretty dirty, but for all intents and purposes, she still looked gorgeous.

"Magic, I think," Noah replied, taking a sip of his bottled water. "Want some?" They were sitting on a bench in the middle of a huge outdoor auditorium that was slowly filling up with people.

She shook her head and leaned against him. "No, thanks."

It felt good to sit down after all the standing they'd been doing. At least all that waiting in lines had given them a lot of time to talk. As he'd discovered the other night, though, they didn't really share many interests. *But how important is that, really?* Noah asked himself. *That's what friends like Meg are for, right?*

Tara began to rummage through her various shopping bags. "I love everything I bought today." Then she laughed. "Or rather, what you bought. You've been such a sweetie."

Noah smiled to himself. He'd been a genius to come up with this idea about the magic show. Not only was the likelihood of an altercation with a kid highly unlikely, there was no shopping in sight.

"We came here for our senior class trip," Tara said, crumpling up the top of her bag and lacing her fingers in his. "Where did you go for yours?"

Uh-oh. "Um, well, we didn't have one." That wasn't exactly a lie. They hadn't had one . . . yet.

"Wow, bummer." She flipped through the map with her spare hand. "What did you say the name of your school was again?"

"Lakeville."

Tara looked thoughtful. "I don't think I've ever heard of it."

"Oh, well, it's, uh, very small. Hey, look!" He pointed to the stage below. A maintenance man was carrying a speaker across the stage. It was a weak attempt at diversion, but it was the best he could do.

She frowned, her gaze darting across the bleachers. "At what?"

Noah shrunk down in his seat. "I thought I saw someone from the Fish Market."

"Ooh, I didn't tell you," Tara said suddenly, her eyes growing wide. "There was a near-drowning outside the restaurant the other day. Thank God Luke was there."

"Luke?"

"The lifeguard. You remember, we ran into him at Blue Baja."

The ponytail guy. "Oh, right. Good thing he was there."

"You bet it is," Tara agreed. "I watched the whole thing. This kid got caught in a riptide, and Luke saved him in the nick of time."

"That was lucky," Noah said absently, his thoughts drifting elsewhere. Suddenly, out of nowhere, his mind focused on his fight with Meg the day before. He didn't like how they'd left things. After he'd toweled off on the beach, he'd had to run off to work. There weren't any hard feelings between them, but he still felt uneasy about the whole situation.

The bottom line was that he didn't want his relationship with Meg to get complicated. And they'd never fought before, so why should they start now?

"Ladies and gentleman, boys and girls, frogs and rabbits . . ." A deep male voice boomed out from the stereo surround system, startling Noah out of his thoughts. Amid a smattering of applause, a man dressed all in white and a woman dressed all in black came onto the stage. They bowed, then began taking props out of a large satin-trimmed sack.

Noah glanced over at Tara. Her eyes were riveted on the act below. *I shouldn't let my fight with Meg take away from my fun with Tara,* he told himself, smiling at her.

"Looks like this could be good, huh?" he said, putting his arm around her waist.

Tara nodded. "Do you think they sell that sack here in the park?" she asked. "It would be perfect for my laundry in the dorm."

The park's nighttime lights were just beginning to come on as Noah and Tara made their way onto the log flume. The ride operator assigned them to a log already occupied in the front by a couple who looked about Noah's age. Noah and Tara stepped into the back, being careful not to slip.

"Okay," Tara said, sitting down on the dry part of the vinyl seat. "I hope I don't get too wet. Here." She handed him a cluster of bags. "Can you make sure these stay dry?"

After a day in the hot sun, getting wet was what

Noah was looking forward to most. "We're in the back. It won't be too bad," he told her, carefully tucking her packages in on the side.

The log bobbed along a few curves before chugging its way up a medium-sized hill. Noah wrapped his arms around Tara, pulling her close and burying his nose in her silky hair. This was the kind of moment he'd been waiting for all day. . . .

As they shot down the first hill, the couple in front of them screamed and waved their arms. Noah laughed, loving the cool night breeze on his face and the free-falling feeling as the log plunged forward.

"Yahoooo!" he cried. He gulped back a second outburst as Tara turned her face toward his.

"You almost broke my eardrum!" Tara laughed, unclenching her fingers from the safety rail to whack him playfully on the chest. "Don't encourage these two in front of us. They're loud enough already," she whispered over her shoulder, her head knocking against his chin. Water sloshed over their feet as Tara snuggled closer. "I wish we had our own log."

"Me too," he said, a ripple of adrenaline zinging through him. He ducked his head around Tara's to glance at the couple she was complaining about. The girl had long blond hair that kept blowing in her boyfriend's face. He was laughing, tickling her. And when they let out a scream as the log dipped down the next hill, they weren't being too loud or anything. They were just having fun.

Actually, they kind of reminded him of Meg and himself.

Noah frowned. Meg. Why did she keep popping into his mind? He'd watched a show once where a psychologist talked about this kind of thing . . . intrusive thinking, she'd called it. Meg was an intrusive thought.

Quit intruding! he thought, squeezing his eyes shut and tightening his grip on Tara. He had the rest of the summer to pal around with Meg. Who knew how long he'd have with Tara?

The ride ended too quickly for Noah. When they climbed out of their log, their clothes stuck to their bodies and their sneakers squished.

Tara made a face as she squeezed some water out of her top. "If I'd known how wet we'd get on this, I never would've gone on it."

Noah checked his watch. "Well, we're going to be leaving soon anyway. . . ."

Tara hastily pulled out the now-soggy map from her back pocket. "I want to make sure we go back to all the shops where I saw stuff that I said I wanted to go back for later," she announced, hauling him down a tree-lined path.

They stopped at a hat shop. "I would just die if you wore this," Tara said, placing a colorful jester's hat on his head.

"So would I," Noah said unhappily. "Wouldn't a baseball cap do?"

"You can get those anywhere. This is special." She gave the little bell on the top a jingle. To

Noah's surprise, she took out a small leather wallet—he hadn't thought she'd brought one. "You have to have some sort of souvenir. And besides, you look really cute in this."

"I do?" Noah asked, peering at his reflection in a mirror.

Tara nodded, then leaned over and kissed him, instantly erasing any objections he might have had. "You do," she said.

Noah adjusted the soft cotton brim, flushing under her gaze. If Tara said he looked cute, then it must be true. After all, she was in college.

She should know.

Noah could still smell Tara's musky perfume as he slipped into his house and jogged upstairs to his room later that night. To his surprise, Meg was sprawled out on her stomach on his bed, leafing through a magazine.

"Hi," he said, taken aback. He tossed his empty wallet on the dresser along with a handful of change and a wadded-up candy bar wrapper. "What's up? You're here kind of late."

"I can't believe you." She flipped the magazine shut and tossed it on the floor.

"What?"

She sat up and crossed her arms. "What day is it, Noah?"

Noah scratched his head. "Uh, Saturday?" He checked his watch. "Technically it's Sunday, since it's after twelve, and—"

"Do we or do we not have a long-standing date at the Rialto on Saturday nights?"

Noah stood there slack-jawed. "Oh, man, Meg. Movie night." For the past few years it had gone without saying that he, Meg, and a king-sized bucket of popcorn with extra butter could be found in the tenth row on the left at Silver Sands' old-fashioned cinema each and every Saturday night.

"Yeah, Noah. Movie night."

He lifted up his hands, then let them drop. "I'm sorry. I guess I was so buzzed when Tara called that I completely forgot. I feel totally lame."

"Your mom told me you went to Busch Gardens with her today," Meg said, giving him a level stare.

Noah nodded, attempting to smile. "I didn't think you'd mind, since we've gone there so many times already."

Meg shrugged. "They add new stuff each year."

"Well, you and I can still go together," Noah assured her, glad to be off the touchy subject of movie night. "I mean, I want to go with you," he amended. "I didn't get to go on half the rides today."

"Hmmm."

Okay, so she was definitely ticked off, but Noah hoped it would blow over. *Just keep the conversation going,* he told himself, *keep her mind off movie night.* "We had fun, though," he said brightly, taking off his watch.

"Well, I know everyone else sure did. All they had to do was take one look at you in your hat."

Noah's hand flew to his head. "What's wrong with this?" he said, taking the cap off. "I think it's cool."

Meg let out a snort. "I suppose Tara brainwashed you into buying that."

"Yeah, right." Noah sat down next to her on the bed. What was her problem? Ever since he'd met the girl of his summer fantasies, Meg had been giving him such a hard time. "What do you have against Tara?" he asked.

"Nothing, except that since you two met your mind has been in a permanent state of off."

"That's not true!" Noah protested. Was it? "Anyway, she wants to meet you, you know," he lied. "Especially now that we're going out."

"You're going out?" Meg asked in disbelief, her mouth dropping slightly.

"Pretty much," Noah told her.

Meg sat there silently. *What is she thinking?* Noah wondered.

"So we'll have to have a get-acquainted date or something," he suggested, although in reality he wasn't quite sure what the three of them would do together.

"Ooh, let me check my social calendar," Meg said sarcastically, thumbing through an imaginary date book. "Oops, I'm all booked. Sorry."

At least she was making jokes. But still . . . Noah let out a small laugh. "Come on, Meg. You're acting like . . . like you're jealous or something."

By the angry glare in Meg's eyes and the stony

106

frown on her lips, Noah realized one second too late that he had said the completely wrong thing.

"Jealous? You think I'm jealous of her?" she asked. "Look, Noah, if you think I'm jealous of some waitress, then you have another thing coming!"

"Don't insult Tara! You don't even know her!" Noah shot back. But to his horror, Meg's mouth began to tremble. He reached over to touch her leg, which she immediately retracted.

"Meg, what is it?" he asked, genuinely confused. "It's like you're mad at me for going out with someone!"

"Don't flatter yourself." Meg flung his Dallas Cowboys football pillow at his head and ran out the door, slamming it behind her.

Noah sighed as he picked up the pillow and hugged it. Something was definitely up with Meg this summer.

He just wished he knew what it was. Because whatever it was, it had to stop.

NINE

"**W**HAT DO YOU think of that one?"
Daphne scrunched up her nose. "I don't know . . . 'sun your buns' seems a little much."

Meg rolled her eyes as her friend held up a cheap cotton T-shirt. "Duh, no. I meant those." She pointed to several Boogie boards that were affixed to the souvenir shop wall. Daphne had talked Meg into accompanying her on a saltwater taffy and suntan oil mission, and Meg had decided her board—the same one she'd had since junior high—could use a little updating. "I kind of like the lime-colored one."

Daphne nodded. "Sure, whatever. As long as it floats, you're in business." She moved over and began thumbing through boxes of candy. "Maybe we should pick some up for Noah. Doesn't he love peanut brittle?"

Noah loved anything with sugar as the main ingredient. Meg was about to nod when a little voice nagged at the back of her head. *He didn't bring you back anything from Busch Gardens. He was too busy buying things for Tara.* "It makes him break out," Meg lied. She knew it was petty, but still, she couldn't help herself.

"I swear that boy gets cuter every summer." Daphne dropped a box of taffy and a bottle of Panama Jack on the checkout counter. "If he had brown hair, he'd be in trouble," she joked. Daphne was a strictly dark-haired-guys-only type of girl.

"You'd have some stiff competition," Meg said glumly after showing the salesclerk which board she wanted.

"Is he still crushing on that waitress you told me about the other day?" Daphne asked as Meg paid for her purchase. The two girls walked out of the store and over to Daphne's white VW Beetle.

"Crushing? I wish." Meg tossed the plastic-wrapped board in the back, slid into her seat, and sighed. "They're an official couple now. He told me last night . . . after he blew me off." She explained what had happened as Daphne pulled out of her parking spot. "I sat there waiting like an idiot for him, Daph. Like, for hours."

"You poor thing!" Daphne turned on the radio. "I never thought Noah would get serious with some girl."

Tell me about it, Meg thought miserably. Every time she thought of the two of them together, her

110

chest constricted painfully. "Tara, Tara, Tara. She's all he ever talks about lately. It's getting kind of nauseating." She twisted a lock of her hair. "I mean, he's totally hung up on her."

"I guess that's natural," Daphne mused. "When you first start going out with someone, everything they do seems great."

"I guess." Meg pressed her forehead against the glass of the window. "I just don't understand what he sees in her, that's all. I never thought he was like other guys. I always thought he'd pick somebody because he liked her as a friend, or because he thought she was cool." She swallowed. "But the only stuff that seems to matter to him is that she's older, she dresses really sexy, and she's got major cleavage." *The exact opposite of me,* Meg added silently.

Daphne gave her a curious look. "Are you sure Noah's taste in girls is all that's bothering you?"

When Meg didn't answer, Daphne poked her playfully in the arm. "If I didn't know you better, I'd say you were jealous."

Meg bit her lip hard, but it was no use . . . the tears began to slide down her cheeks anyway. Ever since Noah had met Tara, Meg had felt powerless, watching their friendship dwindle away by the hour and the chance of a romantic relationship disappear altogether.

"Oh, Meg," Daphne said quietly. "Why didn't you say anything?"

Meg shrugged, wiping away a tear. "I

would've, but . . . but what good would it have done? He's been obsessed with Tara since the moment we got here." Just saying the words out loud made her feel like gagging. "And it's obvious that he doesn't like me in a boyfriend-girlfriend way," she said, her voice squeaky. "He treats me just like he always did. Like a friend. Nothing more."

"Have you ever thought of telling him how you feel?" Daphne asked, making a right turn off the busy main drag.

"No!" Meg said, horrified. "And don't you go getting any ideas." That was all she needed. She could do without Noah's pity.

The sun had begun to slip from its high point in the sky, causing an early afternoon sun glare. Daphne flipped the Beetle's visor down. "Did it ever occur to you that maybe Noah likes you too? And maybe he felt that you'd never see him as anything but a friend either, so he gave up and went after Tara?" She sighed. "You guys would make the cutest couple. I can't believe I never thought of it."

Well, Meg had thought of it. She'd thought plenty. And sure, Daphne's explanation for Noah's behavior sounded good, but Meg doubted it was true. You could tell when a guy liked you—and when he didn't. She stared out the window, the prospect of a long, lonely summer stretching out in front of her, a summer where she'd have to listen to her dream guy sing the praises of another girl every single day.

Why can't Noah see how right we are together? she asked herself for the millionth time.

"Look," Daphne said after several minutes had passed. "Life is short. And summer's even shorter. I say you tell him how you feel. What's the worst thing that can happen?"

"He pats me on the head and tells me I'm sweet but he doesn't like me like that," Meg responded, her shoulders sagging. "And I'm humiliated for the rest of the summer."

Daphne waved her hand back and forth as if humiliation were a minor speed bump on the racecourse of love. "And what's the best thing?"

"That he realizes Tara means nothing to him and he comes to me on bended knee, begging me to be his girlfriend."

"Right." Daphne smiled. "So if you don't say anything, what happens?"

Meg shrugged. "I guess I'm basically your average miserable teenager."

Daphne sailed through a yellow light. "Then you owe it to yourself to say something. Either way you're going to be miserable. So at least give yourself a reason to be." She looked at Meg over the top rims of her purple-tinted sunglasses. "And one last piece of advice: Never put all your eggs in one basket. Sometimes the easiest way to get over one cute guy is to meet another."

That was an idea. It certainly would be easier than telling Noah the truth. Meg was still mulling over Daphne's logic when they peeled around the corner near her house.

"Daph! Watch out!" A guy who looked about their age was cycling down the street. Or rather, he had been cycling a moment earlier. Now he lay in the middle of the road, his lean legs tangled up in the bike spokes, his helmet tilted crazily to the side.

Daphne slammed on the brakes and Meg jumped out of the car.

"Are you okay?" she asked, bending over the cyclist. Daphne hadn't actually hit him, but she'd come dangerously close.

"I think so," the guy said, wincing as he took off his helmet. His eyes and his hair were a rich, deep brown, a sharp contrast to his ashen face.

Meg pointed to his knee. A tiny trickle of blood oozed out. "You're injured," she said.

"I am so sorry!" Daphne exclaimed, hurrying over. "Please tell me all your limbs are still intact."

He nodded. "But I'm afraid I can't say the same for my bike." The front tire rubber flapped loosely in the air. "I don't suppose you guys could give me a lift home? I'm staying at a condo down in Dolphin Head."

"Of course we can," Meg said, giving him a hand up. The color was returning to his cheeks. "That's the least we can do after nearly running you over."

"Don't worry about it." The guy smiled at Meg, revealing big dimples. "Just think. If you hadn't, we never would've met."

Meg smiled back at him. Maybe the summer wouldn't be so lonely after all.

A few isolated pops and shooting-star wheezes sounded off at various points along the beach as Noah walked the short distance to Brilliant Gold on Monday, the Fourth of July. He'd lain pretty low the day before. After the way she'd freaked on him Saturday night, Noah wanted to give Meg plenty of breathing room. Sure, he knew that forgetting movie night was one of his lamer moves this summer. And it wasn't that he felt justified, exactly, but didn't he have an excuse to be forgetful? Falling in deep like with someone wasn't something he'd experienced before. Being with Tara was taking up all the free space his brain had.

Still, his rationale to himself wasn't making things any easier, and by the time he got to the Williamses' door, the gnawing in his stomach had subsided into a dull but determined ache. Noah knew it was up to him to make the first move, but he wasn't looking forward to it.

He pressed his face against the screen door. There she was, sprawled out on the living room couch, a gallon of milk and box of Corn Puffs on the carpet and a bowl balanced on her stomach. Her hair was messy all around her face and her lips were kind of puffy—a sign that she'd just woken up.

He rapped lightly on the door. "Any room in there for an ex–best friend?"

Meg jumped, startled, sending a tiny rivulet of milk dribbling down the side of the bowl and onto her gray T-shirt. Placing the bowl on the floor, she got up and came to the door.

He straightened up and gave her his most appealing smile. It didn't work. Flicking up the door lock, she turned and walked back into the living room without saying a word.

"Hello to you too," Noah said, feeling his ribs tighten as he followed her inside. He took out the small American flag he'd stolen from his mom's petunia planter and waved it in her face. "I'm here to celebrate the heritage of our friendship." He sat down on the love seat. "That is, if we still have one."

She shook some more Corn Puffs into the bowl, ignoring him. "Great," she muttered as only two Puffs fell into the bowl. "I told my mom we were running out. And what's left is soggy."

"I'm definitely not to blame for that," he joked. She arched an eyebrow in his direction. "Am I?" he added, suddenly not so sure.

She propped her feet back up. "No," she said finally. "You're absolved on all counts of mushy cereal."

"What about on all counts of royally screwing up?" He went over and sat next to her. "I'm very sorry about Saturday night," he said softly.

Meg stirred the sloppy mixture in her bowl.

"You know I'd never forget movie night on purpose," Noah told her. "It was just that—"

"I know, Noah. You got totally psyched over Tara and yada, yada, yada."

He shrugged, feeling kind of sheepish. "Forgive me?"

She placed the cereal bowl on the floor and looked up at him. "There's Hungry Jack pancake mix in the top right cabinet. Eggs and bacon are in the fridge." She snapped her fingers. "And ooh, I think I saw a cantaloupe in the fruit bowl."

Noah rose to his feet, a wave of comfort washing over him. "Thanks for giving me a break."

Meg lounged back on the couch. "Don't jump the gun. I haven't tasted your cooking yet."

"Maybe it wasn't such a good idea to eat and bike right afterward," Noah said as they pedaled down Sandpiper Road. His stomach had been feeling kind of queasy ever since they'd left Meg's.

"I told you not to open that extra package of bacon," Meg called over her shoulder. "Just think of all that grease congealing in your stomach. Yum."

Noah cranked up the speed on his mountain bike and pedaled harder.

They rounded corner after corner, matching each other's smooth, even strides. When they reached a flat, traffic-free road, Meg sat back on her seat and tugged impatiently at the strap under her chin.

"I hate these things," she muttered, giving her helmet a plunk with her finger.

"But you look so cute in magenta resin," Noah teased.

Meg cranked up her gears a notch. "At least we both get to look like dorks."

"Speak for yourself," Noah said as they neared the inlet behind their houses.

They coasted their bikes along the narrow dirt path that led to the boat slip, the long, spindly grasses tickling their legs. Even though Noah's family didn't own a motorboat, the slip and the dock that went with it was theirs for the summer.

Noah hopped off his bike and propped it up against the white wooden railing at the end of the long boat landing. Meg did so too, and the two of them walked out on the dock, one of many peppering the inlet.

"Everything looks the same," Noah said, surveying the scene. Large, expensive boats, their names painted on the hull, floated gracefully out of their slips, slow-putting motorboats revved their engines at the dock, and brightly colored Sunfish darted in and out of the paths of their showy sisters. Yellowed reeds grew in the waters that surrounded the dock, dragonflies alighting only briefly before flying off again.

"My legs always feel like jelly after I bike," Meg said, sitting down on the dock. She took a swig of water from the bottle she'd carried with her. Tiny beads of sweat had formed on her upper lip, and her hair was plastered to her forehead.

"I'll rub them if you like," Noah offered.

"Hey, that's right," Meg said, removing her helmet and offering him a drink. "You owe me a massage."

Noah began to knead the firm flesh of Meg's calves. She winced, stiffening her leg. "Ow—I've got a cramp."

Noah improvised, massaging her legs all over. "Does this help?"

"Yeah." She leaned back on her elbows and squirted the last drops of water over her T-shirt, the midday sun heavy overhead. "I could get used to this, you know."

After a few minutes he stopped. "Enough?"

"I suppose." She scratched at a mosquito bite on her leg, looking thoughtful. "I forgot how much I like coming here. The dock's a perfect place to sit and think."

"That's for sure," Noah agreed. He smiled over at her. After a weekend of upheaval between them, he was finally starting to feel comfortable with Meg once again. It was the way things used to be.

The way Noah realized he always wanted them to be.

"Noah?"

"Yeah?"

Meg stared down at the water. "What do you think about us?"

"Us?" he repeated, yawning. Food and sun always made him sleepy.

"You know. How we're getting along and stuff."

Leave it to Meg to read his mind. "I don't like

how we've been arguing." He reached over and squeezed her arm. "But I'm happy now . . . now that we're together and stuff." He placed his hands on the dock, feeling the places where the paint had chipped away below his palms.

"Me too. I've . . . I've missed being with you," she said seriously, her eyes flicking toward him.

Noah put his arm around her shoulder. His relationship with Meg had never been the touchy-feely kind, but it just felt like the right thing to do.

"At the risk of sounding like a cheeseball, it's times like now, when we're just hanging out, that I realize how important you are to me," Noah told her. It was the truth. Knowing you always had a shoulder to cry on—or lean on after eating too much greasy food—was a wonderful thing.

Meg flushed. "I'm glad." She cleared her throat. "Noah, I . . . I have something I want to talk to you about."

"Shoot." He pulled his toes back and forth in the water, loving how it cooled and tingled his skin.

"Well . . ." She paused. "It's, um, well—" She let out a giggle—a rather nervous-sounding giggle. "It's about Tara."

Noah nodded. "I know, I know. You want to know when you'll meet her." He grinned. "It's all taken care of. She's coming over for the fireworks tonight."

Despite the hot afternoon sun pelting down on them, Noah felt goose bumps pop out all over Meg's arms.

"Oh . . . okay."

Noah swatted away a dragonfly. "I told her how we have this awesome spot for watching them on the beach, and she thought it sounded great."

"So you really care about her, then," Meg said, as more of a statement than a question.

He considered this. Everything felt kind of new to him. He was sure he wasn't in love with Tara. But caring? That seemed possible. He nodded. "Yeah, I do."

"Like you care about me?" Meg asked, biting her lip.

That was a weird comment. What did she mean? "Not exactly," he said slowly. "The way I care about you is different. I love—"

Meg turned a sleepy-eyed gaze at him, and for a split second he almost forgot whom he was talking to—or what he was trying to say. He swallowed. "I love knowing that we're always going to be friends. Like, no matter what." Noah shook his head, trying to gain some clarity. "Now, I don't know about you, but I'm ready to hit the beach."

"Okay . . . sure," Meg said.

Noah smiled. He couldn't wait for Meg to meet Tara. Sure, she seemed a little reluctant about the whole thing, but Noah knew she'd get over it.

And then he'd get to spend time with the two

most important people in his summer . . . together at last!

By eight-thirty that evening the intermittent sound of exploding firecrackers was commonplace along the crescent of beach where a dozen or so of the summer families were finishing their communal holiday barbecue. After a sun-filled day of swimming and running and sloshing lemonade, little kids had settled down, willing snugglers in their parents' arms. Waves lapped the shore quietly, almost tiredly, and the sun was slowly sinking into the ocean, leaving the sky bathed in red and orange hues.

Noah and Andy and an eager team of age-ten-and-under helpers had scoured the beach for an hour, dragging back driftwood, dead branches, and whatever else they could find that looked flammable.

"Beth seems really nice," Noah remarked as they dumped a final pile of kindling, looking back to where she sat lighting sparklers for a gaggle of kids.

"She's great," Andy said, gazing with smitten eyes at his new crush. "Of course, she *is* our age, but . . ."

Noah gave him a good-natured shove. Age was something he wasn't in the mood to joke about—he was worried that he'd have a tough time keeping his age a secret from Tara that night, especially considering how many people were there to blow his cover. So part of him was kind of happy that she didn't seem to be in a socializing mood. Another part of him was a little bummed, though.

He glanced over at her. She was sitting by herself, a few feet from the bonfire, a plaid wool blanket tucked around her legs. "So what do you think of Tara?" he asked Andy under his breath.

Andy brushed off some bits of bark that had stuck to his shirt. "Like you said, she's hot. But I haven't really talked to her yet, so . . ." He drifted off.

Noah nodded. As usual, Tara looked perfect. She had on a short denim skirt and a pale blue top, emphasizing her deeply tanned skin. Noah had been psyched to introduce her to everyone, but she didn't seem very interested in meeting his friends.

The evening wasn't going at all the way he'd planned. Meg and Tara had said hello and made small talk for a few minutes, but then this guy Meg had invited, Jeff, arrived, and Meg had drifted off to be with him.

When Jeff had shown up on the beach asking for Meg, Noah had been more than surprised. He'd have thought that Meg would mention she'd invited a guy to the party. Especially a guy Noah didn't know. Jeff seemed nice enough, Noah granted, but still . . .

"Well, catch you later, Andy," he said, selecting a small branch from the pile of kindling and walking over to Tara.

"Later," Andy called after him.

"Having fun?" He sat down beside Tara and handed her the stick. "I found you a good one for roasting."

She took the stick and swirled its tip in the sand. "I'm not a big marshmallow fan. They get your hands so sticky."

"I guess," he said, eyeing her perfectly manicured nails.

A shimmer of blond hair caught his eye across the firelight. Meg had spent the day in shorts and a bikini top, but as the night cooled off she'd put on faded jeans and an oversize navy blue sweatshirt, her hair still damp from a predinner swim. She and Jeff were sitting side by side, talking and laughing.

Noah shoved a plump marshmallow on his stick and spun it in the fire. "Must be nine o'clock," he said, noticing that flares had begun to light up along the shore. Local stores sold foot-long red flares, and at precisely nine o'clock each year, the residents of Silver Sands lit them on the Fourth of July, outlining the beach in red.

Suddenly a burst of high-pitched laughter spilled over from the other side of the fire. Meg's laughter. Noah grimaced—whatever Jeff said had obviously cracked Meg up.

Noah felt a little pang of jealousy stab him in the gut. It was weird, seeing her laugh like that with someone else.

Tara tugged on his arm. "Look! The fireworks are starting."

Noah nodded, pulling her close as a burst of color exploded in the sky, causing a wave of oohs and aahs from the group. Then he glanced back at Meg. Jeff's arm was draped casually over her shoulder, and they both were staring up at the inky black sky, Meg's head resting lightly on his chest.

"Guess the fireworks in the sky aren't the only ones taking place," Tara noted as Jeff bent down and gave Meg a kiss.

"Guess not." Noah wanted to block out the scene that was taking place across the fire. What did he care if Meg kissed some guy? "Maybe we should start our own right here."

"Sounds good to me," Tara purred.

Noah met her lips with his. But as they kissed he found himself opening his eyes and staring up at the red, white, and blue pinwheels as they showered into the ocean . . . and then staring over at Meg. He watched, trancelike, as she kissed Jeff, their faces glowing under the amber flames of the fire. He'd never thought of Meg kissing anyone— or realized how much it would bug him if she did.

Yanking his eyes away, Noah tried to focus on Tara's willing lips. *Who Meg wants to kiss is her business, not yours,* he told himself, putting his energy into his and Tara's kiss.

The thing was, man-made fireworks could be set off at any time.

Heart-made fireworks were a little trickier.

TEN

THE SUN GLITTERED down on Meg's house on Tuesday, its zillion windows sending reflections every which way. When it was this hot this early in the morning, the rest of the day was sure to be a scorcher.

Noah walked across the lawn, kicking the shreds of paper left over from the previous night's fireworks. He'd had a really hard time getting to sleep afterward. For some reason, all he could think about was Meg's lip-locking with Jeff. It was so weird to see her doing that—like bumping into your teacher out at a restaurant, or noticing the priest from church playing tennis in the park. Some things in life you just didn't want to see.

Noah tied Sam's leash to the Williamses' side porch, let himself in with his key, and headed up to Meg's room.

"Yo, Meg," he called, walking through the

empty house. Maybe she was still asleep. Reaching the top of the stairs, Noah headed down the hallway and pushed open Meg's half-closed door.

And he gasped.

He couldn't help it.

"Hey!" Meg snatched a beach towel from her bed and threw it up to her bikini-clad body. "What are you doing?"

Noah felt his cheeks fill with color. He wasn't doing anything . . . except standing there, his mouth hanging open and his hand still clutching the doorknob.

What else could he do? After all, Meg hadn't been sleeping. She'd been standing in front of her full-length mirror, wearing what had to be the skimpiest bikini in the history of swimwear.

"Noah? Hello?" Still holding the towel with one hand, Meg used her other hand to snap her fingers sharply in Noah's face.

Noah felt kind of the way he had when he'd gotten knocked in the head by Andy's elbow when they were shooting hoops the summer before, except instead of seeing stars, all he could see were dots . . . little white dots superimposed over three tiny blue triangles of nylon.

"You're not planning on wearing that in public," Noah stated.

"I think I'll lose the towel first," Meg said dryly, dropping the towel and pulling her hair back into a ponytail. "Did you have fun last night?"

"What?" he asked, distracted. Since when had

Meg looked so incredible in a bikini? In such a tiny bikini? "Oh. Oh, yeah. Great time." Noah sat down heavily on Meg's unmade bed. "How about you and Jeff?"

"He loved it. Said it was the best Fourth he's ever had."

"You certainly made him feel welcome," Noah commented.

"Well, you know, he doesn't really know anyone, and . . ." She trailed off, her mouth forming into a small smile.

Noah decided not to push it. He shouldn't care about what she did with Jeff anyway. He stood up and stuck his thumbs in his belt loops. "So you're going to the beach, huh?"

"Let me see. What could give you that idea?" Meg asked, dabbing some sunblock on her nose. "Was it . . . the bathing suit?"

Noah smacked himself on the forehead. "Oh, is that what you call those little scraps of fabric?"

"You should've seen the one I wanted to get," Meg laughed. "Daphne wouldn't let me."

"At least one of you had some sense." He bent down to stretch his calves—and to avoid looking at Meg in her bikini. "Anyway, Tara's busy today, so we can hang out."

Meg arched an eyebrow. "Is that how it works? When Tara's not free, you can do something with me?"

Noah frowned, not liking how that sounded. That wasn't what he'd meant. "Tara doesn't control me, Meg. I can do whatever I want."

"Oh," Meg responded, pulling on a pair of jean shorts. "I see." She grabbed her beach bag.

Noah groaned to himself. There was that moody tone of voice again. What was the deal with her? "So do you want to hang out or not?" he asked, feeling irritated.

Meg stood in the doorway for a moment, holding her bag. "Yeah," she said after several long seconds. "Of course." Then she walked out of the room.

Noah sighed. He pushed off from the bed and followed her silently down the hall.

He didn't know why Meg was acting so weird, but he did know one thing. He didn't like that she'd had to think about whether she wanted to hang out with him.

He didn't like it one bit.

Some days the sun could be invigorating, but that day it was just hot. The umbrellas lining the beach were like pinwheels of color against the pure blue backdrop of the cloud-free sky.

Noah and Meg lounged lazily under their umbrella, making the most of their little oasis. The cooler was stocked, the music was on, and they'd already been down to the water twice to cool off.

A flock of seagulls flew overhead, coasting on the sea breeze. Below them, Sam ran in and out of the water, barking at waves that had the audacity to get his paws wet. It was a designated Pet Day at

Silver Sands. Anything that barked or meowed was welcome.

Noah lay on his stomach, so sleepy he could barely keep his eyes open. The sound of the surf always did that to him.

Meg sat next to him in her portable beach chair, her legs sticking out in the sunshine, deeply engrossed in a magazine article. She held a bottle of iced tea steady between her thighs.

"Is he the one for you?" she murmured. "The guy who sits behind you in class asks if he can be your lab partner. You—"

Noah opened one eye and squinted over at her as she grew quiet, nibbling on her pen and scanning the various choices.

"Don't tell me you're taking another one of those lame quizzes," he said as she checked off a response with a flourish. "They're so weak."

"No, they're not. In fact, they can be extremely self-revealing, if you're willing to be honest with yourself." She chewed her lip as she read the next one.

"What?" Noah propped himself up on his elbows. "Is that a hard one? Ask me."

Meg shook her head. "This is really designed for girls to take, Noah. I don't think you—"

"Ask me," he insisted, his interest doubled now. "Go on. Prove to me this isn't the lamest thing since they installed that drive-through at the doughnut shop."

"'You have had a crush on a—'" She broke off.

"You know, Noah, you're right. These things really are cheesy." She tossed the magazine carelessly on the beach towel and flexed her legs. "Whaddaya say we go for a swim?"

"No way! This is a total attempt to blow me off when I know I'm right." He went for the magazine, rolling away from Meg's grasping hands. "Let's see," he said, turning the pages. "Where were we?" His finger moved down the list of questions. "Here it is. 'You have had a crush on a male friend for a long time. You can't go on any longer without telling him how you feel. Your approach is to: (a) tell him point-blank how you feel, (b) never tell him—can you say "end of friendship"?—or (c) hope that he figures it out but if he doesn't, you're prepared to spill.' Hmmm. Interesting question." Noah looked up at Meg. "So which is it?"

"What do you mean?" she asked, suddenly extremely fascinated by the cooler's locking mechanism.

"Which would you pick?" Noah asked, genuinely curious now. He knew she had some good guy buddies back in Philly. *Does she like any of them?* he wondered.

Meg was about to reply when her eyes focused on someone on the beach.

"Jeff!" Meg began to wave so frantically, Noah thought it was a wonder her arm didn't pop out of its socket. "Jeff! Over here!"

"Meg!" He came jogging over, a cardboard box containing four hot dogs and two large paper cups

132

of soda in his hands. "Hi!" he said, smiling down at them. He was wearing a pair of droopy swim trunks and worn leather sandals. Noah had to admit that the guy was built. Still, did Meg have to be so ridiculously excited to see him? *You'd think he was Leonardo DiCaprio or something. And what am I? Chopped liver?*

"I can't believe we ran into you!" Meg exclaimed, patting the towel beside her. "Why don't you join us?"

Noah hoped he'd say no. After all, they were having a perfectly good time on their own. . . .

"Well, for a minute," Jeff responded, dropping down. He nodded to the food. "My brother's waiting for me."

"Joshua?" Meg smiled. "I'd love to meet him."

"I'd bring you over, but he's too busy horsing around with some kids he met this morning." Jeff craned his neck up in an attempt to spot him. "They're probably terrorizing the little old ladies who sit near the water. They skim their boards so close to the shore. But I can't complain. He's a pretty cool little dude."

"So, are you having a good time here?" Noah asked politely, secretly wishing Jeff would scoot on back to his brother. Sure, he seemed like a nice enough guy, but, well, Noah liked it better when it was just him and Meg.

Or, of course, if Tara were here it would be more fun, he told himself, suddenly realizing that he hadn't thought about her all morning.

Jeff shrugged. "The beach sure is beautiful, but I've been a little bored, to be honest. Daphne and Meg are the first people I've met."

Meg giggled. "Tell Noah that joke you were telling me and Daph last night. About the repairman and the housewife."

Noah tried to look interested.

Jeff laughed. "I never tell the same joke twice—I always end up forgetting something. Besides, it wasn't that funny."

"Yes it was!" Meg insisted. She reached over and squeezed Jeff's muscular arm, her fingers leaving pale impressions on his lightly tanned skin. Noah felt himself involuntarily tense up. "You told it really well."

"It's easy to be funny when you've got an appreciative audience," Jeff said, standing up. "I'd better get going. Josh turns into a real cretin without lunch."

"I'm glad you stopped by," Meg told him.

"Yeah." Noah forced a brief smile.

"I'm glad too," Jeff said. Then his voice dropped a notch as he leaned over Meg. "I don't know if you're free tonight, but . . ." He let his words drift off.

Meg flipped her hair over her shoulder. "There's a great fried oyster and clam place on the strip. We could—"

"Pete's?" Noah blurted out. That was their place!

"Noah and I go there a lot," Meg explained to Jeff.

"Sounds great. But only if you let it be my treat.

I owe you for coming to my rescue the other day."
He smiled.

"But—" Noah began.

"What?" Meg asked, turning to him.

He flushed under her gaze. *Yeah, Noah, but what?* he thought. He shrugged sheepishly. After all, if a nice enough, somewhat boring guy wanted to take Meg out for fried oysters as a thank-you, what was the big deal?

No big deal at all.

None.

"Good one!" Noah called as Meg leaped for and caught the bright yellow Frisbee, splashing back down in the surf.

After Jeff had left, they'd ate the tuna fish sandwiches they'd packed, and then spent the afternoon cooling off down by the water. Noah was happy—this was just how he liked it. Just him and Meg and the ocean. No distractions. No Jeff.

Meg bowed grandly and sailed the Frisbee straight to his hands.

Noah tucked the disc under his arm and then sent it flying back toward her. "Flying saucer straight ahead!" he called. But his aim was off and the Frisbee went right over her head, landing at the feet of a blond guy sitting on a towel, dark sunglasses shading his vision. He looked to be about their age and was already well on the way to developing a killer tan, with the muscular body to show it off. Noah hated guys like that.

Meg jogged over to him. Noah watched as the guy picked up the disc, stood up, and handed it back to Meg . . . along with a much bigger smile than necessary.

Oh, please! Noah thought. *Meg will see right through his cheesy act.* But to his supreme distress, Meg returned the guy's smile with an even bigger one.

Jeez! Since when is Meg, like, the biggest flirt on the beach? "C'mon, let's play," he called in a too-loud voice, shooting the guy a pointed glare. Hadn't making small talk with Jeff been enough for one day?

Meg leaned over and said something to the guy—something that made him laugh. He took off his sunglasses and said a few words back. Noah cursed himself for not being better at lipreading. Then Meg turned around and walked back. Without warning, she zinged the Frisbee at Noah.

"I wasn't ready," Noah complained, bending over to pick it up. He looked up and noticed that the guy was now watching them play. For effect, Noah did a little spin, flinging the Frisbee under his leg.

"Show-off!" Meg called with a laugh, easily catching it.

Watching her through the eyes of Mr. Sunglasses, Noah became conscious once again of how good Meg looked in her bikini, her long hair twisted at the nape of her neck.

Noah jogged over to her. "You want to do

something else?" he asked in a low voice, in case the guy was eavesdropping too. "Go in the water for a while?"

"Okay." She pulled off her hair clip and they ran into the surf. Noah resisted the urge to shoot Meg's observer a victory glance.

The water felt amazing, and Noah could've jumped waves with Meg for hours. He'd barely gotten enough when Meg tugged on his waterproof sports watch twenty minutes later.

"Don't you have to go to work?" she asked, bobbing beside him and tilting her wet head to the side.

"Oh, man," Noah said, realizing he had to leave immediately if he wanted to have any hope of making it. They hurried back to shore, Noah barely taking time to dry his face before turning to go back to the house.

"Come on, Meg, I don't have a lot of time," he said. She hadn't made a move to leave the beach.

"You go ahead. I'm going to stay for a while."

"But . . ." Noah looked around them, his eyes traveling back to the Frisbee guy. He was still there. Still watching. Suddenly Noah really didn't want Meg to stay on the beach without him. "But I'm going," he said, as if this were a good enough reason for her to leave too.

"Okay." She wiped her face with a towel and picked up her magazine. Noah just stood there, frozen, looking at her. Meg squinted up at him, shielding her face from the sun with her hand.

"You're going to be in trouble if you don't get moving."

"C'mon," Noah said, frowning. He pointed up toward the sun. "It's getting late. What do you want to do down here by yourself anyway?"

Meg pushed her sunglasses atop her head. "It's only four-thirty, Noah. I think my mommy will let me stay out until five."

Noah tried to bite back the annoyance that was chewing up his stomach. At least with Jeff he knew Meg was in semidecent hands. But this guy . . . who knew what his story was?

"I'm just trying to look out for you. We've been out all day and . . . and . . ." He paused, trying to come up with something. "In case you've forgotten, you end up looking like a lobster if you're not careful."

Meg waved a bottle of suntan lotion in his face. "Can you say sunblock? Besides, the sun's at its weakest right now. And its most beautiful."

She was right. The sun was slowly sliding its way down from the zenith of midday, and the water underneath glistened in its warmth.

Noah folded his arms across his chest, helpless. "Okay, fine." Once he was gone, he knew, he just *knew*, that Blondie was going to come over and ask Meg to play Frisbee. Or worse yet, do something totally lame, such as ask if he could bum a can of soda from the cooler. Or maybe even ask if he could put lotion on Meg's back.

But Noah knew he couldn't stand there any

longer without looking like a complete idiot. "Bye," he said to Meg. She gave him a small wave. Noah dusted the sand off his legs and, catching one last glimpse of Meg's streaky blond hair, turned to go.

No way would Meg bother talking to that guy, he decided. She didn't know him, she didn't need to know him, and she sure as heck didn't want to know him.

She didn't need another guy.

She had him . . . and Jeff, of course.

ELEVEN

"S O THURSDAY NIGHT is SeaFest," Tara said on Tuesday evening, placing a parsley garnish on the fisherman's platter in front of her. Behind her the deep fryer was sputtering oil, and the sounds of reggae music competed with the huge fans that whirred in all four corners of the Fish Market's kitchen.

"That's right," Noah said, remembering the giant banner proclaiming Silver Sands' annual crustacean bash that he'd passed on his way into work. He carefully placed four garden salads on his tray. "I went with my parents once, but I don't really remember much."

"It's a lot of fun. They've got some really great jazz and blues acts scheduled this year." Tara picked up her tray and balanced it on her shoulder. "What do you say we check it out?"

"Sure. If you want to," Noah said, preoccupied.

All he could think about was how Meg's date was going.

"Is something wrong?" Tara asked, bringing her head close, her glossy hair caressing his cheek. A week earlier he would have loved having her special attention, but that night, well . . . he just wasn't into it.

"No, nothing's wrong," Noah said. He reached over and kissed her cheek. Then he had a sudden idea. "I don't suppose you'd feel like going over to Pete's for some fried oysters after our shifts end?"

"Oysters?" Tara wrinkled her nose. "In case you haven't noticed, Noah, we work in a seafood restaurant. Going to an oyster shack isn't how I want to spend my free time." She laughed. "What possessed you to want to do that?"

He shrugged. "Just a craving, I guess."

The next week flew by for Noah. He couldn't believe how quickly time was passing this summer. It seemed like only yesterday he'd said good-bye to his friends in Roanoke, and here it was getting toward the middle of July already. Of course, he'd had a few things to occupy his time. Or, more accurately, one big thing. Tara.

The last few days had been a whirlwind of dating activity. Since Meg had met Jeff, Noah had decided to throw himself into spending time with Tara.

They'd zoomed around on Jet Skis. Shopped. SeaFested. And, of course, gone to work. Noah's days had been so jam-packed, he'd practically had to schedule time to brush his teeth.

This day, though, Noah was on his own. Tara had gone to visit her father in D.C. So, without thinking, Noah immediately headed over to Meg's.

The truth was, he'd realized when he woke up that morning, he was having major Meg withdrawal. Not seeing her had actually affected his moods. He'd been crabby these past few days, and he and Tara had been having stupid little arguments.

Yep, he definitely needed a small break from Tara. And he certainly needed some serious Meg time.

Noah smiled as he made his way to Meg's house. Maybe they could go crabbing out in Chincoteague—the weather was gorgeous. Or they could go to the Sea Oats—those blueberry pancakes were always calling him. He whistled as he walked up to her door, the sun twinkling overhead.

Mrs. Williams greeted him. "You just missed her, Noah. She and Daphne and their new friend Jeff went to the mall." She shook the soapsuds off her hands and opened the door to let Noah in.

"Oh," Noah said, surprised. He'd just assumed she would be there. He thought for a moment. "I kind of wanted to talk to her. I guess I'll just leave her a note."

Mrs. Williams waved him toward the stairs and returned to the sink of dirty dishes. "You know the way."

Taking the steps two at a time, Noah jogged up

to Meg's room. Then he picked up a neon yellow pad and grabbed a pen from her desk.

Long time no see! When you get back, meet me on the beach, he scrawled, signing his name with a flourish. Then, as an afterthought, he added, *I miss you.* It was true, after all.

As he ripped the note off the pad and tossed it on the desk, his eye fell on a white envelope with handwriting he didn't recognize. A Philadelphia postmark dated a week ago was stamped across its front. Curious, Noah picked up the envelope. As he did, a glossy picture slid out and dropped onto the floor. Noah crouched down to see what it was.

A radiant Meg stared back at him. Her hair was piled atop her head in a perfectly achieved messy bun, her lips were all pink and glistening, and she was wearing a slinky black gown held up by the thinnest of jeweled straps and a wrist corsage of one sunflower. She looked beautiful.

Noah refused to say the same for the guy who stood beside her, his right arm snaked around her waist, his left clasping her arm. So what if he had thick brown hair, piercing blue eyes, and a tall, lean physique?

If this had been anybody else, Noah would have given the picture a casual glance, said something complimentary, and moved on.

But this wasn't just anybody. It was Meg. On a date. With a guy who looked, well, sort of cool. He stared at the photograph, trying to shape the guy into some dweeby drip. A pity date.

It wasn't working.

Why hadn't Meg mentioned him? He'd thought that Jeff was the first guy she'd liked.

That's stupid, man, he told himself. *Of course Meg's liked other guys.*

The realization was profoundly disturbing.

Tossing the photo aside, Noah tugged at the letter that was wedged inside the envelope. For a moment he felt a twinge of guilt as he unfolded the sharply creased paper. He wasn't the kind of guy who pried. He respected his friends' stuff.

But, he rationalized, he couldn't be prying. Prying was something your parents did to make sure you weren't stashing liquor under your bed or growing marijuana plants in your room. But making sure you didn't date a total psycho—now that was what a good friend was for. "And psychos can really deceive you. They look completely normal," Noah declared to the empty room.

Feeling totally in the right, Noah read the letter. He learned that the guy's name was Billy. He worked in the golf clubhouse at some country club in Philadelphia, was taking two college prep classes over the summer, and missed Meg a lot. Blah, blah, blah. Noah rolled his eyes as he read detail after detail of extravagant pool parties filled with people named Stockton and Whitney, and Billy's list of reasons why he thought his father should buy him a new car, preferably a BMW. *Please,* Noah thought. The guy was a big snobby bore.

Completely wrong for Meg.

Noah took another look at the photo. The more he studied it, the more he realized that the guy wasn't so hot after all. His hair was thick to the point of being bushy. His eyes weren't piercing . . . in fact, he was almost cross-eyed, if you looked closely enough.

I know why she didn't say anything. He sounds like a pretentious jerk—and he looks like an even bigger one. She'd probably dumped him after the dance, and now here he was writing to her, hoping for some response. No, *expecting* some response.

Noah laughed to himself. He knew how to bring Mr. College Prep down a peg or two. With a steady hand, he neatly colored in one of Billy's oversized (and no doubt capped) teeth a nice shade of Bic blue, then put the letter and photo back on Meg's desk.

He grinned. He loved having good ammo to rag her with.

It was one of those perfect beach days that you dream about all year, or see in movies or on postcards. The sun was high in an electric blue sky, warming the crests of the ocean crashing below, and the beach was a buzz of Frisbees, sand castles, and sunblock-covered toddlers.

Noah grabbed the far edge of his yellow-and-orange board and pulled his body up so that his torso was sticking out of the water. He'd spent the past hour diving into wave after wave, only now beginning to feel the first whispers of fatigue. He'd swum out to just past where the waves crashed, where he could still rise and fall on the waves and not risk getting overturned.

Noah held on to the board loosely now, resting his cheek on its hard, wet surface, one eye lazily scanning the shore for his friends.

A familiar-looking blonde in a purple racer-back suit setting up camp next to his mom's umbrella caught his attention.

"Meg!" Noah waved her over. "Come on out!"

She tossed her sunglasses on her beach towel and ran down to the water's edge.

Noah always admired how Meg didn't tiptoe into the water and squeal over how cold it was. She just splashed right in.

"Hey," she said a couple of seconds later, surfacing beside him. "The water's awesome." She wiped the hair from her face.

"I feel like I haven't seen you in so long," Noah said, splashing her.

"You haven't. You've been too busy making goo-goo eyes at Tara."

Noah reached down to dunk her, but she was too quick and moved out of the way.

"Let me have that," she said, grabbing for the board.

Before Noah knew what was happening, Meg dove beneath the surface.

"Hey!" he cried as ten fingers began to tickle his legs. He tried to get away, but Meg wasn't having any part of it. Without warning, she came at him from behind, flinging her arms around his neck and wrapping her legs around his waist, her hair hitting his skin.

Then she rubbed her head against the back of his neck and laughed.

"Cut it out!" Noah said, bumping his head lightly against hers, but he was laughing too. "You're going to be sorry." He swam inland, still gripping the board, with Meg still glommed onto his back. The weight of her body made it harder to swim, but Noah was a strong swimmer.

Still, he couldn't give Meg a free ride all the way to the beach. First he needed to play with her a bit more.

In a sudden movement, Noah quickly spun over, dunking Meg completely underwater. "No fair!" she sputtered, bobbing up beside him, her legs tangling with his. "You're lucky I had my mouth closed."

"For a change," Noah teased, splashing her.

"Oh, yeah?" Ducking away, Meg swam to the other side of the board, using it as a shield against him as his initial splashes turned into an all-out splash war. When each of them had swallowed enough salt water to fill a ten-gallon tank, Noah let go of the board and made a time-out sign.

"I guess we can share." Noah extended half of the board to her.

Meg flung one lightly tanned arm around it. "Gee, thanks," she replied, putting her head down on the board and turning to look at him.

Noah laid his head down too. They were so

close that Noah could see the light smattering of freckles that had appeared across her nose. Droplets of water had formed on her skin, and Noah reached over and touched a particularly big one that was threatening to fall in her eye.

"A bug?" Meg asked, blinking. Her eyes glistened back at him.

"Mmm-hmmm," Noah said softly. The competitive spirit he'd felt for the past ten minutes had disappeared.

She yawned, her toes fluttering in the water. "I feel so tired all of a sudden."

"That's no good. You've got to save your energy," Noah told her as they floated over the top of a good-sized crest.

"Why?"

"All that writing you have to do," he said, poker-faced.

"Writing?"

Noah laughed. "You know. The letter you've got to send before wittle Billy has a wittle meltdown." Noah grinned over at her, expecting a grin in return.

Instead Meg gasped, her eyes growing wide. "You? You were the one who defaced my prom photo?"

"*Defacing* is a bit harsh. I just, uh, colorized it," Noah explained, continuing his flutter kick.

"It was already in color!" Meg spat out, letting go of the board. The shift in weight nearly caused Noah to capsize.

"Don't tell me you're mad," he said, incredulous. What was the big deal?

149

Meg's face was white with anger. Scary anger. "No, I was mad before. I just didn't know who to be mad at. I *thought* it was weird of Billy to do something like that."

"Oh, and it's not weird to sign the letter 'My heart misses you'?"

"You read the letter?" Meg screamed.

Noah swallowed nervously. "Um, yeah. So?"

Meg slapped her hand down on the water. "So it wasn't yours to read!"

"It was just a dumb letter," Noah mumbled, his cheeks flushing. "It wasn't like there was anything important in there," he added in an attempt to downplay what he'd done. "It can't mean that much to you. You've never even mentioned his name—or told me you went to the prom! And I told you," he reminded her.

By now the water was shallow enough for their feet to touch. "You're right, Noah. I didn't mention him. Because *I* don't go around blabbing nonstop about the people I go out with!"

"People?" Noah exclaimed. "You mean there's more?"

Meg put her hands on her hips, ignoring him. "Who gave you the right to go through my things?" she demanded.

Noah couldn't believe how upset she was. "Maybe you shouldn't leave your stuff out in the open," he said, avoiding the question. Deep down Noah knew he shouldn't have read her letter, but he hadn't expected her to have such a bad reaction.

They'd never had to hide stuff from each other before.

The board began to float away.

"I'd hardly call my own private mail in my own private room leaving things out in the open!" Meg yelled, her eyes blazing. A couple of kids in water wings swam hastily away from them. "Maybe you shouldn't just stroll into my room when I'm not around."

"Maybe I shouldn't," Noah shot back, stung.

"Maybe you shouldn't stroll into my room period," she said hotly.

"Don't worry," Noah snapped. "I won't."

With an angry flip of her wet hair, Meg pushed through the water and stomped up to her beach towel. Noah watched as she shoved on her sunglasses, pulled on a T-shirt, and stormed toward her house.

With a heavy heart, he swam over to retrieve the board and headed slowly toward shore. He thought Meg would have found the whole thing funny. He'd had no idea she'd go so mental on him.

A couple of guys nearby laughed as he came out of the water, dragging the board beside him. "Trouble with your girlfriend, huh?" one of them said.

"What? No. A friend," he answered through clenched teeth. Or maybe an ex-friend. By the look on her face, he wasn't too sure they'd ever be on speaking terms again.

"Really?" One of the guys craned his neck to watch as Meg strode through the sand. "She's hot."

Noah didn't know whether to punch him or not.

TWELVE

"IF YOU DON'T stop pacing, we're going to have a permanent path ground into the carpet," Meg's mother chided, tapping her fingernails on the end table.

"I just can't believe him," Meg muttered angrily, doing another about-face. "The nerve! To come in here and touch—no, deface—my private property!" She was seething. How dare Noah touch her prom photo! The fact that Billy was nothing more than a guy from biology lab, someone she'd dated only a few times, was irrelevant.

"Did he really do such a bad thing?" her mother asked, putting down the crossword puzzle she was working on.

Meg scowled. She hadn't given her mother all the details when she'd stormed in from the beach— her anger was still too raw. "Mom, Noah came in here when I wasn't home, went into my room, read a personal letter, and, to top it off, made Billy's teeth a nice shade of Bic blue." She folded her arms. "So you tell me."

Her mother winced. "That does sound bad."

"See!" She flung herself down on the couch. This was really the last straw. Day after day she'd let herself be taken for granted. Whenever he needed to talk, she was there. If he needed advice, she doled it out. *I even helped him get dressed for his date with Tara!* she thought angrily, sinking her nails into a nearby pillow.

Tara. What had first made her incredibly sad was starting to make her feel incredibly angry. She would no longer sit around and make herself so available to Noah when it was clear that not only would he never love her back, he didn't even appreciate her friendship.

And that gives him no right to interfere in my life, she thought grimly.

It was about time he got the message.

"We need to talk," Meg barked, banging her fist repeatedly on the back door.

"Okay, okay," Noah said, clicking off the phone with Tara and tearing his eyes away from *Entertainment Tonight.* He frowned as she came storming into the living room. He'd been dying to talk to her ever since their fight that afternoon, but it didn't look as though she'd cooled off any. If anything, she seemed more fired up than before—if that was possible. "What'd I do now?" he asked wearily.

Meg folded her arms tightly across her chest. "I've been doing a lot of thinking since our little *incident*, Noah," she began. "And I came up with a little list of things I want to talk about." She whipped out a piece of notebook paper from her back jeans pocket.

"You've made a list of things to rag on me about?" Meg had flipped out even more than he'd thought.

She sat down in the old maple rocker and began to methodically rock back and forth. "Not exactly." She poked the paper with her finger. "I'm talking boundaries here, Noah."

"Boundaries?" Noah chewed his lip, trying to figure out where she was going with this. "Like what?"

"Let me make this simple for you. When we were little, remember how you would come over and build sand castles in my sandbox?"

"Yeah . . ."

"And do you remember how I used to knock them down with my shovel?"

"You were a regular wrecking crew." He laughed. "I used to get so angry!"

"Right . . . until my mom pointed out that it was my sandbox, and if I wanted to knock down sand castles, be they yours or mine, I had every right to do so. You had your own sandbox to play in."

He nodded. "But I'm not sure I get the analogy."

She cleared her throat. "That was a boundary

my mom set. A boundary you weren't supposed to break." She settled back in her seat. "It's time we set some new boundaries."

Noah was mildly amused by the turn this conversation had taken. And Meg looked so cute when she was serious like this. "Okay, okay. I promise not to knock over any of your sand castles. I won't even go in your wading pool," he joked.

Meg didn't look pleased. "May I continue? For starters, I need my privacy. No more popping in my room any old time."

"But why?" he asked. Sure, she'd said those very words on the beach, but he hadn't thought she'd really *meant* them. Meg's bedroom was like his second home. "I promise I won't snoop again. Scout's honor." He held up four fingers.

"You're not a Scout."

"But—"

Meg was unmoved. "Not unless you knock first."

"Okay, sure," he said, shrugging.

Meg narrowed her eyes. "And my right to privacy includes my mail. It's a federal offense to tamper with someone's mail, Noah."

He rolled his eyes. "I think that applies to mail that's still in the mailbox."

She raised her eyebrows. "Can I finish?"

"You need your privacy. All right," Noah agreed quickly, willing to say anything to cut this conversation short. "Is that it?"

"No." She looked at her list. "You can't just assume I'm free at the drop of a hat."

As though he ever did that! "If agreeing with you will make you happy, fine."

Meg rocked harder, the chair's rockers thumping on the hardwood floor underneath. "I don't want you to agree with me simply for the sake of agreeing," she said angrily. She took a deep breath. "I'm totally serious here. I've had it. You're taking complete advantage of me, and I won't stand for it anymore."

Where was this coming from? All he'd done was read a letter! "I think you're overreacting, Meg."

She shook her head. "I'm not overreacting. Whenever Tara's around, I'm invisible. Then, when she can't make time for you, you suddenly think, 'Gee, I wonder what poor old Meg's doing.'" She crumpled her list into a ball and threw it at him. "I'm sick of being used!"

Was that what she thought? That he used her? *I have been spending a lot of time with Tara lately.* He nodded slowly—he understood now. "So you're jealous that I've been hanging out with Tara so much."

"No, Noah. I'm not jealous of her." She glared at him. "Why would I be jealous of a girl who has an insensitive user of a boyfriend?"

Ouch. Noah averted his gaze. *That was harsh.*

Meg leaned forward, placing her elbows on her thighs. "Now, back to the boundaries."

"I thought you were through," he said in a small voice, pointing to the discarded list.

"Not quite." She allowed a smile to appear.

"But I'm glad you brought Tara up, because it's the perfect lead-in to my next point. Intimate details of our sex lives should be kept to ourselves."

Noah made a face. "That's no fun!"

Meg folded her arms. "Well, that's the rule."

"Who says you get to make all the rules? Don't I have a say?"

"Sure. Go ahead." Meg waited.

"Well, I don't have anything now," he admitted after a few uncomfortable, silent moments. "I didn't know you were coming here to give me a list of dos and don'ts." He began to feel worried. "But what if I have this weird girl problem that only you can answer? I don't think that last one is a good idea."

"Don't you get it?" Meg burst out, startling him in the process. "I don't want to get involved in your love life," she explained, her voice growing frustrated. "I don't want to hear how your dates went, I don't want to know what they wore, and I especially, *especially* don't want to hear how they kiss or . . . or anything like that," she finished, waving her hands around.

"But that's the kind of stuff I want to tell you," he said, confused. "I mean, you're my best friend. I've always told you everything on my mind."

Meg sighed. "I'm used to telling you everything too, Noah. But this summer—" She looked at him, her eyes weary. "This summer it's different. We're older. We're not little kids anymore."

"Just because we're getting older doesn't mean that things have to change between us," Noah said stubbornly. "We'll always be best friends."

Meg looked as if she was about to say something, but she was silent for a few moments longer. "Look, I've got to go," she finally said, abruptly standing up and leaving Noah completely baffled. She paused at the doorway. "I hope at least a tenth of what I'm telling you sank in, Noah."

"Oh, I'd say at least half," he deadpanned, turning on the outdoor porch light.

But she wasn't in the mood for jokes. "I'll see you, okay?" She let the door shut softly behind her.

As Noah watched her walk the short distance to her house, he played back the conversation in his mind, Meg's sentences blurring and fading into single words. *Boundaries. Privacy. Tara.*

Clearly he hadn't been making enough time for Meg. Lashing out at him was her way of expressing this.

I'll definitely hang out with her more from now on, he promised himself, opening up the refrigerator. *And then she'll see that's she's wrong. Things between us don't have to change just because we're getting older. We can still be best friends.*

Yep. That was him and Meg . . . best friends forever.

THIRTEEN

NOAH CHEWED THOUGHTFULLY on his pen. Action? He loved action. But the only action film playing at the Rialto had gotten a one-star rating. Bad sign. He skipped down the remaining choices. Alien invasion flick: too juvenile. Disney animated movie: okay, but he wasn't really in the mood for singing porpoises. Romantic comedy about two people who are meant to be together except they just don't realize it: perfect, just what he was in the mood for. Noah circled that one with his pen as he walked next door.

After their talk the night before, he was determined to make this evening extra special for Meg. It hadn't been hard to see past her out-of-control spiel on boundaries. Noah knew she didn't *really* care about stuff like keeping her room off-limits or any of those other half-baked issues she'd been going on about. She didn't really want anything between them to change. No, Meg was upset because they hadn't spent enough time together. Just like him, she was having serious withdrawal. And it was obviously making her moody.

That's why this night, their first movie night of the summer, was so important. Noah had showered, shampooed, and even gone the extra mile of splashing some of his dad's aftershave on his face. Once this night was over, things would be back to normal and Meg would be fine. He was sure of it.

"Oh, hi," Meg said, waving him in with a tube of lipstick when he rapped on her bedroom door.

Boy, she's totally into tonight, Noah thought. She'd even dressed for the occasion, he noted, admiring her white denim shorts and the sleeveless cotton shirt that tied at her waist.

Noah flopped down on her bed, spreading the newspaper out in front of him. "Okay, *Summer Love* starts at seven. If you hurry, we'll—"

"I can't go tonight," Meg cut in.

"Huh?" Noah looked up from the paper.

Meg blotted her lips with a tissue. "I can't go tonight. I have plans with Jeff."

Noah sat up and rubbed his ears. "For some funny reason it sounded like you said you had plans with Jeff."

"I do," she said. "He's taking me to the arcade."

"What?" Noah flung the newspaper onto the floor. "You're giving up movie night to go play video games? With . . . with *Jeff?*"

Meg chose a pair of pearl earrings from her

jewelry box. "If you'd bothered to ask me today instead of just assuming I was free—"

"But—" Noah protested.

"—I would've been." She stuck the backs on the studs and turned to give Noah a bare-shouldered shrug. "Sorry."

"Sorry?" Noah repeated, dumbfounded. He tried to think of a better comeback, but his brain was still trying to compute the fact that Meg was passing him over for a . . . a guy. "But what about movie night?" he demanded, his voice thick.

"What about it?" She picked up her purse.

"It's tonight!" he shouted. Was she on drugs or what?

"Oh. I didn't think we were observing movie night anymore, Noah," Meg said primly, sliding her feet into her platform leather sandals. "Remember how you conveniently forgot about it last time?"

"I told you I was sorry," he said, pouting.

"Well, I'm sorry too," she said. "But I thought after last night . . ." She shook her head, looking completely fed up. "Didn't a word of what I said sink in?"

"Well, yeah!" He fought back the urge to shake her. "That's why I'm here!" he went on angrily. "I took extra pains to get ready tonight, and you're— you're going out with some guy?" He stopped to catch his breath. "And an arcade? What kind of dumb thing is that to do on a date?"

"You and I have gone to the arcade lots of times," Meg pointed out.

That was beside the point. "Yeah, but we weren't on a date!"

Meg glanced at her gold bangle watch. "I don't have time to argue semantics with you. Jeff's picking me up any second."

Noah stood up and noisily stomped over the newspaper. "You know, I could've gone out with Tara tonight, but noooo, I told her I had plans with you!"

"Well, there's a first," Meg said sarcastically.

"What's that supposed to mean?" he demanded. "I'd never blow you off for Tara . . . well, at least not on purpose. I—"

"Like I said yesterday, I'm not always going to be here at your beck and call. You can't just blow me off all week and then expect me to want to hang with you at your convenience."

"Yeah, but . . ." Noah knew when he was sinking, and he was sinking fast.

A horn beeped outside. Meg glanced out the window. "Gotta go."

"So that's it? You're leaving?" Noah asked.

"Yes, Noah, I am," Meg told him. "Get a life, will you?"

And before he could reply, she was gone.

Noah sat down on Meg's antique double bed. Picking up one of her seashell-appliquéd pillows, he punched it angrily with his fist. How could Meg blow him off this way and then act as though it was no big deal?

Like some crazed maniac, he blasted down the

stairs and back to his house, his cheeks flaming. When he got inside, he pulled Tara's number out of his wallet and angrily punched in the seven numbers.

"Hi, Tara," he said, trying to bring his voice back down to size. "It's Noah. Turns out I am free tonight after all. . . ."

Tara dabbed her mouth with her pale pink napkin and took another delicate bite of cheesecake, her eyes skipping around the well-heeled crowd of diners. "I can't believe we got in here without a reservation," she said, a small, beaded table lamp casting a romantic glow on her skin.

She looked fantastic. A short-sleeved red silk turtleneck slid over her body like a wetsuit, and underneath the white linen tablecloth rested a pair of deeply tanned legs nicely exposed by a short white skirt.

Noah tugged on his tie in vain. He guessed the price of dining at Mollusk was strangulation. This wasn't the kind of place he would have picked, but Tara hadn't been willing to drop her plans with her friend Amy unless Noah "made it worth her while," as she'd put it.

Noah refused to consider how rude that particular comment was. He was too busy forcing himself to have the best date in the history of dating. Still . . .

Give me Pete's oysters and Marnie's ice cream any day, he thought, almost tasting the succulent fried oysters he and Meg had always enjoyed.

165

This place was another story. Other than a tasty clam chowder, the overpriced food was too fancy for Noah's taste. Right now he was staring down at a small dark square in the middle of his plate, covered with strings of red and orange gel. It was a sin that they could destroy chocolate cake this way. *But that's not the point,* Noah told himself. *The point is, this is better than any old night with Meg.*

He smiled at Tara as his knee brushed against hers. But his mind continued to wander. He wondered what Meg and Jeff were doing at that moment. Were they battling each other at the pinball machines? Were they soaring over the beach in the old-fashioned Ferris wheel Meg loved so much?

"Noah!" Tara waved her fingers in front of his face.

"I'm sorry," he said, flushing.

"You seem preoccupied," Tara told him, frowning.

Jeff was probably busy trying to show off his skills on games Meg had mastered summers ago.

Don't think about them. Meg blew you off tonight, Noah reminded himself, his mood turning sour. In defiance, he reached over and squeezed Tara's hand.

"I, uh, was just thinking. Maybe on our next day off together, you could come over and rent a movie or we could go clamming. My house is right near an awesome crabbing shoal, and . . ." He broke off, seeing Tara's face fill with displeasure.

"Clamming?" She played with the hair on his wrist. "I'm not really into that kind of thing."

"It was just an idea," Noah said quickly. "If you have some other suggestions . . ."

Tara smiled up at the waiter as he bustled over with a steaming pot. "More coffee?" he asked, bowing slightly.

"No, thank you."

"Just the check, please," Noah said, patting his pocket to make sure his wallet was there.

"Well, I did hear they just opened a new mall about twenty minutes away." She giggled. "You wouldn't believe all the stuff I've got to get before school starts up again. I want to redecorate my dorm room, and . . ."

He stared down into his coffee cup, barely listening. He didn't even like coffee. "Whatever you want, Tara."

And even though it was barely ten o'clock, Noah was suddenly feeling very, very tired.

"Well, thanks for dinner," Tara said as Noah pulled up in front of her condominium later that evening.

Dinner had been painfully long, and after driving around town for about an hour, Noah couldn't think of anything else to do except take her home. He shifted the car into park. "Sure. My pleasure."

Every other time he'd dropped her off, he'd used his best leading-man move, peeling one hand from the steering wheel and draping it casually over her shoulder.

But not this night. This night he just wanted to go home.

"Aren't you going to turn off the headlights?" Tara murmured silkily, edging closer in anticipation.

Noah shifted self-consciously in his seat. "Um, well, I'm kind of beat, actually." He turned to her with a small apologetic smile. He'd wanted this kind of moment for so long that it was hard to believe he was actually passing it up. "I guess I'd better get going," he said.

Tara jerked back, obviously offended. "I guess you'd better."

Noah leaned over and gave her a quick kiss on the lips. "Good night."

She opened the door and got out. "Good night," she said curtly.

Noah waited until she walked inside before driving away. There was no denying that was the absolute worst kiss they'd ever had. And the worst date.

But, funny enough, he didn't even care. Tara would get over it, and if not . . . so what? Her attitude was starting to get on his nerves. Maybe dating a college girl wasn't worth the bragging rights he'd thought were so important.

Suddenly summer was getting a lot more complicated.

FOURTEEN

"NO, NO, NO! Oh, man." Andy flung himself back on the faded denim couch as the Orioles, bases loaded, struck out at their last at bat. "That's what they get for trading two good pitching prospects for that clown!" he shouted, shaking his finger at the television.

Noah nodded, absently shoving some Famous Amos chocolate chip cookies in his mouth. They tasted dry and stale.

"The season is over. Over!" Andy shouted. "We're never gonna make it to the World Series if we keep playing like this." He craned his neck to look at Noah, slumped in the Astleys' easy chair. "Can you believe this baloney?"

"It's sad," Noah mumbled, his mouth full of cookie.

Andy stared at him. "What's sad is you. What's with you today?"

"Huh? What do you mean?"

"You. You're a mess." Andy gestured to Noah's grass-stained Ziggy Marley T-shirt, wrinkled shorts, and rumpled hair. "I've never seen you look so bad."

Noah shrugged as a cookie crumb fell off the side of his face. He was trying to concentrate on the game, he really was. He loved the Orioles. But he was too preoccupied.

"Did you see Tara last night?"

"Uh-huh," he said. But even the thought of Tara's full lips and short skirt couldn't perk him up. All he could think of was Meg . . . and Jeff. Meg and Jeff. Jeff and Meg. *Did she kiss him last night? The way they kissed on the Fourth of July?* He couldn't get the image out of his mind.

"Did you guys have fun?"

"Who?"

"You and Tara," Andy said impatiently, throwing a pillow at him.

"If you call spending two weeks' salary and getting the car door slammed in my face fun, then yeah." He shook his head when Andy looked at him inquisitively. He didn't want to talk about it.

Shrugging, Andy picked up the remote and began flipping through the channels. "Beth and I had a great time last night," he said. "We went down to the arcade."

"The arcade?" Noah sat up. "Did you see Meg there?"

"Yeah, she was with that guy Jeff. He seems cool."

"What were they doing?"

Andy gave him a funny look. "You know, the usual arcade stuff. Eating cotton candy, playing games." He leaned back on the couch. "It figures, though. Just when we saw them, Jeff had won Meg a huge teddy bear at the dartboards, and Beth wanted one too. I spent ten bucks, and all she ended up with was a tiny Pooh key chain." He smiled. "But we still had fun. Beth's very cool."

Cotton candy, video games, dartboards, Meg . . . it would've been great. But instead, while Meg was busy having a good time without him, Noah had been stuffed into a dress shirt and tie, eating asparagus risotto.

"They weren't holding hands or anything, were they?" For some reason he couldn't explain, he really needed to know. "Meg and Jeff, I mean. Were they?"

Andy let out a low whistle and smiled. "I knew it had to happen sooner or later."

Noah felt his pulse quicken. "What? What had to happen?" he demanded.

"That you'd finally realize Meg is the perfect girl for you."

"What?" Noah dropped the box of cookies on the carpet.

"It's time to admit it, Noah," Andy said slowly, as if he were speaking to a seven-year-old. "You guys are meant to be together. Everyone in Silver Sands knows it but you."

Andy was seriously losing it. How had he come up with something so ridiculous? Noah let out an exasperated sigh. "What's wrong with you? Meg and I are friends. That's *all*," he said. "Friends. Buddies. *Amigos*. Pals. Besides," he added, "I've already got a girlfriend. Remember?"

"Then why are you asking me to describe any action that went on between Meg and Jeff?"

"I was just curious, that's all," Noah said. "I mean, she *is* our friend, Andy. I'm interested in her welfare."

"Well, she looked one hundred percent okay last night."

"Good!" Noah declared. "I'm glad. I think it's great that she's dating a nice guy like Jeff." He frowned under Andy's doubtful gaze. "Really. I'm totally happy for her."

"If you say so," Andy said, his expression dubious as he turned toward the television and the seventh inning.

"I do," Noah said to Andy's back, folding his arms. He was just being a good friend, nothing more, he told himself.

He focused his attention on the game and shoved some more cookies in his mouth.

There was still just one problem: Why did he feel so lousy?

The old wooden dock felt hard under his back, and as Noah curled his arms under his head, it occurred to him that he could get some wicked splinters lying the way he was.

Not that it would matter. At least pulling out splinters would give him something to do. The days were dragging by in sweltering monotony. What at first had stretched before him like mouthwatering candy now seemed like eternity. When Noah wasn't dragging himself off to work, he was busy trying to find some new way to entertain Tara, who had grudgingly "forgiven" him. And when he had a spare second to visit Meg, she was always out. Now that Meg had Jeff, Noah felt as though he barely saw her.

As he lay there on the dock, the events of the previous weeks crystallized before his eyes, suddenly becoming clear to him for the first time. He remembered what Meg had said on the day of their "boundary talk."

She was right, he realized, sitting up. *I* did *take her for granted.* But how could he have helped it? Meg had always been there for him. It wasn't until she'd disappeared from his Silver Sands life that he realized just how much she'd been there for him. And how much he really needed her.

Noah sighed. Could Andy have been right? Could he actually be—

"Hey!"

Noah looked up as Meg walked out to the end of the dock. She looked really pretty, dressed in a pair of beige shorts and a white halter top, her long hair cascading down her back.

"What are you doing out here by yourself?"

Meg asked, sitting down beside him. "Where's Tara?"

Noah shrugged. "At the mall or someplace. I was just vegging." He glanced back down the dock. "Where's Jeff?"

"He's at the beach with Daph and some other people." She swung her legs out over the filmy water. "I felt like being by myself."

Noah nodded, understanding the feeling. "Join the party."

They sat together in silence, staring out over the bay. Except for the sound of a couple of ospreys calling to each other and the water rippling quietly beneath their feet, the day was quiet and still.

Noah looked over at Meg. Her skin had a faint, sheer glow, and she smelled like vanilla pudding.

"What?" she asked, touching her hair self-consciously.

"Nothing," he said, actually feeling his cheeks flush. Blushing when he spoke to Meg—this was a low point in the history of their friendship.

But suddenly all Noah wanted to do was look at her, to drink her all in. He missed her so much. Summer just wasn't summer without Meg in his life. His daily life.

But I don't know how to fix things, he thought sadly. Noah wanted things to be how they used to be, before Tara, before Jeff . . . before everything got so complicated.

"I think it's going to storm," Meg said, inter-rupting his thoughts. Noah stared up at the sky. It had turned a deep purple-gray, and the trees that lined the shore were whipping in the breeze that had risen, their leaves blowing inside out.

"Maybe we should head home," Noah said, standing up.

Meg hopped to her feet. "Do you think we'll make—"

As if it had been holding its breath until that very second, the cloud above them burst open, drenching them with huge, warm raindrops.

"Come on!" Noah cried, grabbing her hand. Laughing, they ran down the dock as the rain began to pelt their backs. "Why didn't you bring an umbrella?" he shouted as they raced through the swamp grass, the sharp blades stinging his bare legs.

"Why'd you pick today to hang out at the dock?" Meg answered, gasping as they neared Noah's house. Shaking off as much water as they could, they squeezed into Noah's kitchen, slamming the door behind them. Sam ran back and forth, barking.

"We're drenched!" Noah said, shaking his head the way Sam did after he went swimming.

Meg giggled. "It came down so fast!" They peered out the kitchen window. The driveway had turned into a lake, and the unfortunate souls who'd left their sunroofs open while they spent the day at the beach were in for a rude awakening when they returned.

Meg stepped back from the window, where a

small puddle of water had formed at her feet. "I can't believe I'm saying this after how hot it's been, but I'm freezing." She shivered.

Noah kicked off his soggy sneakers. "Wait right here." Moving as fast as he could without slipping, he grabbed two fuzzy beach towels from the linen closet and hurried back to the kitchen, tossing one to Meg.

"Thanks," she said, her teeth chattering as she wrapped the towel around her shoulders. Even though she had two rivers of mascara running down her face and her lips were the color of diluted ruby red grapefruit juice, Noah thought she'd never looked more beautiful. He tried to picture Tara under the same circumstances.

It wasn't pretty.

"Remember that storm we got caught in last year in Chincoteague?" Meg asked, sitting down at the kitchen table. "At least we have towels now."

"Yep, we got soaked that day." Noah smiled at the memory.

"I wish we could spend more time together," Meg blurted out, squeezing the water from her hair. "I really miss you."

Noah stared at Meg, locking eyes with her, amazed and relieved that she felt the same way. "Me too."

Meg broke their gaze, looking down to the ground. "But you're with Tara and I'm with Jeff. . . ." Her voice trailed off.

You're with Tara and I'm with Jeff. Tara's with

Jeff and I'm with you. . . . Suddenly everything was clear, as if the rainstorm had lifted the cloud from Noah's brain.

"I've got it!" he told her, throwing the towel aside.

"Got what?"

"How we can see more of each other and still keep our respective boyfriend and girlfriend."

"How?"

Noah slapped his hand on the table, amazed he'd overlooked the obvious for so long. "We'll start double-dating!"

Meg didn't respond for a moment. "Double-dating?" She ran her fingers through her wet hair. "I don't know, Noah. That might be a little weird."

"Why? No, it won't," he said, answering his own question. "Look, we both want to spend more time together, but we only have so much time to see each other and Jeff and Tara. So what better way to do it than to all hang out together?" He paced back and forth, getting excited about his idea. "It'll be perfect! You'll get to know Tara, I'll get to know Jeff, and we can hang out like old times."

Meg leaned forward. "Do you really think it would be fun?"

Noah sat down next to her. "Of course it would! And with our schedules, I don't see any other way for us to see each other more. Do you?"

Meg cast her eyes down for a moment, then looked up at him. "No. No, I don't."

Noah smiled. "It's settled, then. Are you guys free tomorrow night?"

As Meg nodded, Noah noticed that her lips were still quivering from the rain. He picked up his towel and draped it over her shoulders.

"I'll plan everything, if that's okay with you," he said as a million possibilities whizzed into his mind. A double date! How could he not have thought of this before? This was the perfect solution to all their problems.

"Okay," Meg said. She smiled at him.

Noah reached over and patted her face dry. Double-dating was definitely the answer.

He was sure of it.

FIFTEEN

CAPTAIN SWANK'S WAS the most popular miniature-golf place in Silver Sands. Noah and Meg had played there lots of times. Tara, however, had apparently never played miniature golf at all.

"Is this how I hold it?" she asked, holding the club as though she were a baton twirler in the Macy's Thanksgiving Day Parade.

Noah sighed and moved behind her, encircling her waist with his arms. "Try to grasp your left thumb with your right hand, and interlock your right pinkie with the finger next to your left thumb," he instructed, moving Tara's hands into position. For some reason the softness of her hair and the nearness of her body did nothing for him that night. In fact, he didn't even feel like touching her.

"I never knew this was such a technical game!"

Tara laughed, swishing her short skirt against his hips.

Noah smiled weakly. The truth was, Tara was really starting to get on his nerves.

He'd been so sure that a double date was a great idea. And perhaps it was, in theory. But nothing had gone right that night. At the pizza place the conversation among the four of them—when any was going on—had been forced. Tara had made it clear that she had no interest in getting to know Meg, and Meg soon returned the favor, talking only to Jeff.

Tara seemed to hate everything that night. She'd disliked the pizza, saying it was too oily. She'd thought the waiter had an attitude. And when she'd come out of the bathroom after applying a fresh coat of makeup, she shuddered with horror at being subjected to such substandard facilities.

Noah didn't know what to do. He felt stuck with Tara . . . at least for the night. Still, he couldn't help wishing that it was just him and Meg playing miniature golf. Alone.

"Oh, it's a very technical sport," Meg commented sarcastically. "I hear they're thinking of adding it to the next Olympics."

Noah shot her a warning look. Sure, he realized that Tara was annoying, but the last thing he needed was for Meg and her to get into an all-out fight. Besides, what did she need to make snide comments for? She had Jeff. The nicest, most polite guy in Silver Sands.

In other words, a big pain.

"Thanks for the sound bite," Tara quipped. She whacked her yellow ball, sending it through a metal loop and straight into the hole.

"Looks like you whipped us on that one," Jeff said, scribbling down everyone's score. "Let's get a move on—it's getting late."

Noah groaned inwardly. Jeff probably wanted to get some alone time with Meg. Just the thought of the two of them kissing suddenly made Noah sick to his stomach.

He trudged on to the next hole with everybody else. The trick to this one was to shoot the ball along a narrow wooden beam through a pirate-ship tunnel and into the hole—the patch on a pirate's eye.

"Your turn, Meg," Jeff said, tapping the rubber putting mat with his club.

Meg lined up her red ball and whaled on it, smacking it into the side of the ship, where it bounced off the side and landed in the grass. Watching her, all Noah could think about was how impossibly cute she looked in her cotton tank top and jean shorts, her hair in a ponytail.

"Almost," Jeff told her. He turned to Noah. "Do we count that?"

"No," Noah replied, his eyes still focused on Meg.

"Why not?" Tara demanded.

Meg raised an eyebrow. "Did we count the ball you shot in the pond a few holes back?"

Tara crossed her arms. "I told you. That kid on the other hole distracted me."

Meg picked up the ball and slammed it down on the mat. "Shot number *two,*" she said, whacking it again. This time it went through the tunnel and dropped into the hole.

Meg smiled victoriously. Noah smiled back at her. *Did she always look this pretty?* he wondered. Or was it something about this night?

When everyone had played their shots, they moved on to the next hole. A family of four was still there, so they had to wait.

"So, Tara," Jeff said, smiling at her. "Are you psyched for senior year?"

Noah shot him a look of pure panic.

She smiled back. "I'm only a sophomore."

"Oh." He shook his head. "You look a lot older."

"Really?" she asked, apparently flattered.

Noah felt his entire body tense up.

"Yeah. Trust me, none of the sophomores at my high school look anything like you," he said.

Tara's brows lowered. "*High school?*"

Noah was unable to speak. *I'm toast,* he thought, his cheeks flaring red.

"Oh, look, they're done," Meg said hurriedly, throwing her ball down on the rubber putting mat.

"Yeah, Boundbrook High," Jeff explained. "Where do you go?"

Just shut up, Jeff! Noah screamed inwardly.

"I went," Tara said thinly. She spun to face

Noah. "Did you know he was in high school?"

Noah swallowed, his palms beginning to sweat. "Well, uh, yeah."

Then her eyes narrowed. "Don't tell me you're in high school too!"

He leaned on a nearby statue of a shipwreck for support. "You could say that."

Tara paced back and forth, ramming her golf club on the concrete sidewalk. "So you're telling me that I'm on a date with, what, a junior?"

"A senior," Noah clarified.

Tara let out a strangled laugh. "A senior."

She yanked up her ball and shoved her club at Noah. "Take me home. Now."

"We're in the middle of a game, Tara. I—"

"The game is over!" she shouted.

Jeff had turned white. "Hey, I had no idea—"

"Forget it," Tara snapped, her eyes glowering at Noah. "Are we going or what?"

Noah looked from Tara to Meg and Jeff, who stared back at him with worried glances. "I can't just leave them," he said under his breath.

"Well, I can." She stormed off in the direction of the parking lot.

Noah just stood there, smiling uncomfortably at them. He couldn't let Tara leave like that—he still had to see her every day at work for the rest of the summer. But then again, he didn't really feel like going after her. Plus he wasn't too into the idea of leaving Meg and Jeff alone. . . .

"It's okay, Noah," Meg told him. "I'll call my

183

dad. He'll come and get Jeff and me when we're through."

"Yeah, we'll be fine," Jeff agreed. "I'm sorry, man. I didn't realize Tara didn't know how old we were."

Noah sighed. "Yeah, well, she would've found out sooner or later."

As Noah walked toward the parking lot, he realized he didn't even care that things were over with Tara.

Especially when he thought about the way Meg had looked at him as he left, her eyes filled with concern.

Breaking up is never easy, especially when you're the one getting dumped. But Noah took it all in stride. "I thought you wouldn't go out with me if you knew the truth," Noah confessed on the drive home.

"You were right." Tara had had a chance to cool off, and she wasn't as angry as Noah had anticipated. "Who knows, in a few years we might be right for each other," she said, patting him on the leg.

Noah was silent. At this point he seriously doubted that. Tara was not his type—he'd learned that much.

Tara took her house keys out of her purse. "And you shouldn't have lied to me about her either."

Noah blinked back at her. "What are you talking about?"

184

Tara's lips curled into the smile that had attracted Noah in the first place. "Just a friend? I don't think so. If any of my friends ever looked at me the way you look at Meg, I'd be doing some serious soul-searching real fast."

Noah's mouth dropped open, his heart beating incredibly fast. He wanted to tell Tara that he didn't have a clue what she was talking about.

But suddenly, sickeningly, he thought he might.

He was in love with Meg.

SIXTEEN

NOAH STARED AT the ceiling, the slow whir of the fan dulling his frenzied brain as the morning sunlight crept over the horizon. Nothing was working. He'd gone through the starting lineup of the Carolina Panthers. He'd made a list of every place he wanted to visit before he turned twenty-five. He'd even calculated how many pizzas he'd eaten in the past year, including their respective toppings.

But all he could think of was one thing.

Meg.

He kicked at his bedsheets, making them even more knotted, if that was possible.

Tara was right. Andy was right. Heck, everyone and their mother was right. He was completely, one hundred percent, head over heels in love with Meg. He'd just been too stupid to see it.

That was why his life had felt so empty since they'd started fighting.

That was why it made him sick to his stomach to see her with another guy.

Was he too late? Was it possible that she really cared about Jeff? That she'd never love Noah back?

Noah bolted upright. No, he wasn't going to let her go. Not now. Not after everything they'd gone through. He had no choice: He had to win her heart . . . his own depended on it.

Noah hugged his pillow, trying to imagine how he could bring up the subject. After all, he couldn't exactly just knock on her door and say, *Hey, Meg. I've been doing some thinking, and I think we should hook up. How 'bout it?*

No, they were best friends. The situation required deft handling.

It had taken him eleven years to figure out that Meg was the girl for him. He wasn't about to screw it up now.

"Whose idea was it to get one of these chairs?" Daphne asked no one in particular, dog-paddling in a small circle before pulling herself up out of the water and climbing into the large plastic seat.

"Yours," Andy replied from where he was treading water, giving her a splash.

"Oh, yeah." She closed her eyes, letting her feet dangle over the chair's edge. "Now if I only had a piña colada, this really would be the life."

Noah was busy fooling around with the new wooden disc he'd picked up at the local surf shop the other day. Between Daphne's floating chair, the various multicolored Boogie boards, and the inflatable inner tubes they'd dragged out, Noah and his friends had assembled a small flotilla, just past where the waves were breaking.

And Noah had decided this would be the day. There was no way he was going to let another minute of the summer go by without telling Meg exactly how he felt about her. Noah couldn't hold it in any longer. He felt like he was going to burst as it was.

Meg, on the other hand, looked perfectly serene. She lay completely still, floating on her back. Only her toes and the palms of her hands fluttered, keeping her afloat. He was just about to swim over to her and suggest that they go grab a bite to eat when she flipped over and began treading water.

"You guys are acting like wimps," Meg scolded, brushing back a clump of hair. "I'm going to go jump waves." She swam inward with sharp, graceful strokes.

Noah handed his disc to Andy. "Hold this, will you?" He swam after her until the water was shallow enough for his feet to reach the sandy, shell-filled sea bottom. Meg bobbed a few feet away from him, and they jumped wave after wave. Normally it was fun, but this time it felt more like a chore. Like an obstacle.

"Great day, isn't it?" he said awkwardly, the bracing sea air ripping through his hair and making his skin above the water chill.

Meg brushed off a dragonfly that had perched on her forearm. "Yep."

Noah swam closer, close enough to see the flecks of light reflected in her blue eyes. "Meg?"

Her shoulders ducked into the water, and she looked right at him. "Are you bummed about Tara? You look so serious."

Noah swallowed, trying to get his courage up. "No. I wanted to tell you that I—" He paused. "Well, you know that we broke up and everything." They jumped together as a wave came crashing in.

Meg tilted her head back. "Well, yeah, Noah. I figured as much. Are you all right about it?"

Noah faltered for a moment as he stared into her eyes.

"Yeah. But I wanted to tell you . . . I need to tell you . . . that—"

"Watch out!" a little boy to his right shrieked.

Noah turned as a giant wave crested over his head and he swallowed some water. He began to hack.

"What was that you were saying?" Meg asked, surfacing cleanly next to him.

Noah spit into the water.

"Lovely," Meg said with a laugh, swimming away.

They had drifted several hundred yards away from their friends, and as Noah did the sidestroke alongside her, his eyes gravitated to the old pier, not too far in the distance. He had a sudden idea, and his eyes met Meg's in an unspoken challenge.

They began to race. Meg was a solid swimmer,

and before long she was a good six feet ahead of him. Noah kicked harder, pulling his body forward with each strong stroke of his arms.

He'd never been so glad to see the old pier in his life, and as he neared it he made a last-ditch effort to pull ahead. But Meg had already touched the saturated wood in victory. Now she was leaning against one of the wooden support beams in knee-deep water, gasping for breath.

"Good race," Noah managed to say, slogging toward her.

"You too," Meg wheezed, leaning her head against the timber, her stomach muscles heaving. She laughed, and he laughed too. It felt like old times again. Just the right atmosphere to say what he needed to say.

Sunlight from the pier overhead filtered down through the wooden slats, casting shadows on the foamy ocean crests. Meg's face was dappled with rays of light and speckled with shadow, and her dripping body glistened, a strand of seaweed wrapped around her shoulder. She looked at him now with eyes bluer than the sea. Never had Noah seen Meg looking more beautiful than she did at this very moment. So he did the only thing he could think of.

He placed his hands against the beam and kissed her, the sound of water lapping against the wood posts of the pier masking the thunderous beats of his heart.

As their lips melted together, a million niggling

thoughts went through Noah's head. *What if she hates this? Will this kiss mean the end of our friendship?*

Will the fireworks ever end?

Before he had time to worry about anything else, Meg pulled away, leaving him breathless. Suddenly he was afraid she was going to make a joke or, worse, tell him how absolutely disgusting what they just did was.

"Meg?" he asked tentatively, reaching out to touch her face. Then, more assured, he whispered, "Meg."

"Noah, I—"

"Are you guys coming?" Andy yelled from down the beach, waving his arms.

"We need you for the volleyball game!" Daphne's voice rang out.

Meg turned and waved. "Be right there!"

"Meg, wait," Noah said, desperate now as she started to slosh toward their friends. "Meg, what's wrong? I didn't mean to scare you. It's just that you look so beautiful, and I've been trying to tell you that—"

"What? What are you trying to tell me?" Meg asked, her voice filled with hurt. "That just because you're through with Tara you're ready to give me a thrill now?"

What? How could she think that? "No, Meg. Listen to me. I—"

"Because if you think I've been waiting around for you to break up with Tara, you're wrong." Her eyes filled with tears. "I'm not some silly girl you can kiss and then walk away from, Noah . . . or someone who's interested in catching a guy on the rebound. You can't use me to satisfy your raging hormonal lust, or whatever it is that's possessed you this summer, and expect me to grin and take it."

"Can you just cool off for a second?" Noah asked, reaching for her. "You're not even giving me a chance."

She shrugged him off. "Just forget it, okay?" Meg pulled the seaweed from her shoulder and flung it at him. Then, wiping her eyes, she turned on her heel and began hurrying down the sand to their friends.

It was a good thing that the pier was there, because if it hadn't been, Noah's jelly-filled legs would have crumpled, sending him sinking into the water. He leaned against a beam and squeezed his eyes closed.

Forget it? How could he? Kissing Meg was like liquefying his heart.

As if in a dream, Noah put his fingers to his lips. After all these years, Noah had kissed Meg Williams.

And she had left him standing in the surf. Alone.

SEVENTEEN

NOAH GAVE HIMSELF a neck massage, cursing the afternoon sun that blazed overhead. He figured that he'd probably picked the hottest, sultriest day possible to sit his sorry butt down on the pier's weather-beaten planks and give himself a pity party. But he didn't care. In fact, he was glad. He deserved every sweat-filled moment.

Glassy-eyed, he stared out at the water. Every little lap, every wave seemed to whisper *loser, loser, loser* as they came slowly in, then crashed on the shore.

That's a good parallel for my life, Noah thought miserably. *I started slow, then crashed.* Except it wasn't so bad for the waves. They could keep trying and trying, over and over, all day and night.

Noah didn't have any chances left.

He looked glumly over at his companions on the pier, the sight making him sigh even more heavily. A bunch of senior citizens wearing fishing caps and short-sleeved cotton dress shirts laughed and talked as they cast their lines off the pier.

Maybe that would be him one day. An old guy in a baseball cap, chewing tobacco and spitting it into the water, reminiscing about the good old days when he still had a friend named Meg. No doubt he'd still be a bachelor. An old bachelor. If he was so clueless that he'd missed seeing that Meg was the perfect girl for him, he'd never be able to find anyone else. He didn't want anyone else.

He flicked a clump of sand off the pier, watching as it scattered into granules in the wind.

I've made such a mess of things this summer. Why was I so blind? He gazed down at the beach below, seeing nothing, hearing nothing, feeling nothing.

The only reason he even noticed the redhead in the strawberry pink bikini was that she was waving like crazy and walking straight for him.

Noah lifted his hand in a listless wave.

"Hi!" Daphne said, staring down at him. "Where are the fish?" she asked, looking around for a nonexistent bucket. Then she pulled off her sunglasses. "Hey, you look awful."

"Thanks." He dropped his head in his hands. "I really made a mess of things, didn't I?"

"What do you mean?"

Noah sighed. "Come on, I know Meg must've told you."

"Well . . . ," Daphne started.

"I was just so blown away that a college girl like Tara would give me the time of day that I didn't see what was staring me right in the face," he confessed, not caring that he was opening up his heart like a littleneck clam. He didn't care about anything anymore.

"Don't go all pitiful on me, Noah," Daphne said, sitting down beside him and kicking her legs back and forth over the water like a little kid. "It's not like she's with anyone else."

"What do you call Jeff?" Noah asked dejectedly.

"Uh . . . my new boyfriend?" Daphne offered, her brown eyes twinkling.

Noah snapped his head up so fast that his neck hurt. "Your what?"

"Jeff and I are going out now," Daphne explained.

"He is? You are?" Noah was stunned. "But—"

Daphne put her arm around him. "Let me explain it to you. See, Jeff really liked Meg. And I mean, who wouldn't? She's terrific. But he liked me too. So since Meg was single and I had someone back home, he went for her."

"What a guy," Noah muttered.

"Then I decided I couldn't deal with having a boyfriend who lives six hours away, and Dave agreed. So we broke up. Just for the summer," she clarified. "And Meg and Jeff had already agreed that they were better as friends than as a couple . . . leaving him free to date me!" Daphne finished gleefully.

For a moment—a brief, short-lived moment—Noah was psyched. Then cold reality slapped him in the face. "I'm glad that things worked out for you, but I'm still stuck in the realm of the losers." He sighed. "Meg doesn't believe that I really care about her."

"Well, I can tell you're sincere, but I don't count," Daphne told him, giving his arm a squeeze.

"I really love her, Daph," Noah said, not even surprised that he'd said the words aloud. "I don't know what else I can do." He rubbed his eyes tiredly. "And it has nothing to do with being on the rebound. Nothing! I know Meg inside and out . . . there's no one else like her." He paused. "Maybe you could put in a good word for me," he said, somewhat cheered by the idea. "You know, tell her what I've said and stuff?"

Daphne looked doubtful. "I can try, but there's no guarantee. She needs to hear it from you."

Noah nodded sadly. Daphne was right. But how could he tell Meg how he felt when she didn't even want to speak to him?

Daphne patted him on the back. "Things will work out, Noah. I know they will."

"Easy for you to say." He swallowed, his throat tight with emotion. "You didn't see how mad she was."

Daphne stood up. "It'll be fine. Just stay positive."

"How can you be so sure?" Noah asked, squinting up at her.

She smiled. "Because love always comes through in the end."

*   *   *

Noah sincerely hoped that they hadn't run out of the seared scallop special as he hurried back to the kitchen later that night. He'd just taken six orders for it, and at eighteen dollars a pop, he was counting on some big tips. He needed something to lift his spirits.

He jumped back as Tara came out the other swinging door. "Noah, table sixteen requested you as a waiter. I took care of the drink order already."

"You're sure they want me?" Noah asked dubiously, wondering who it could be. Lots of the staff had repeat customers, but he hadn't been on the job that long.

Tara smiled. "Positive."

"Okay. I just have to put this in." He ran back to the kitchen, gave Phil his order, picked up three salads and cruets of oil and vinegar to deliver to table four, and was out again.

Noah was glad that working next to Tara wasn't awkward. If anything, they were getting on better now that they weren't a couple. And apparently Tara had already moved on—he'd heard her going on about Luke the lifeguard with one of the other servers.

Table sixteen was a cozy booth, tucked in between a large wooden statue of a buccaneer and an antique display of life preservers.

Probably my mom and dad in a parental attempt to cheer me up, Noah thought, only slightly cheered by the possibility. Or maybe Andy had brought Beth, a scenario that didn't cheer him at all. Not that he begrudged his friend a happy love life, but he didn't need to witness it that night.

Noah put on his happy-server smile as he approached the booth. "Hi, I'm Noah, and I'll be your—" The words faded as he stared down into the amused faces of Daphne and . . . Meg.

She wore a loose cotton dress patterned with tiny pink and blue flowers, and her hair was held back on the sides with thin blue barrettes.

Daphne gave him a wink.

Noah felt like one of the fish in the restaurant's aquarium, gulping for air.

"Our . . . ?" Meg prompted.

"Servant," he got out.

Meg looked at him quizzically. "Oh, really? Well, in that case—"

"Server," he corrected quickly. "Your server."

She flipped her menu shut. "I'll have the fried shrimp with a baked potato, sour cream, no butter."

Noah scribbled every word down, proof that she was indeed speaking to him again. "Salad dressing?" he asked, poised to write down ranch, Meg's favorite.

"How's the ranch?"

"Very good."

"That's what I'll have." She handed him her menu.

"Make that two," Daphne said, snapping hers shut.

Noah backed away from the table. "I'll be right back with, uh, your salads."

He spent the next hour running back and forth,

making sure Meg had everything she needed. Extra sour cream? No problem. Another refill of Coke? But of course. Noah was so accommodating, he checked himself in a mirror just to make sure he hadn't actually turned into a pretzel.

At one point in the evening Noah took a breather against the kitchen counter, letting the huge portable fan blow over his sweaty self. His brain began to process the night's events for the millionth time.

Meg had come to the Fish Market and requested he wait on her.

He rolled that thought around and around in his mind. He must have stood there for an awfully long time with a sappy expression on his face, because before he knew what was happening, the salad girl was waving a salad in front of his nose as though it were a plate of smelling salts.

"But this is French," Noah said, staring at the thick red dressing.

She exhaled slowly. "I know what it is, Noah. It's the salad you ordered ten minutes ago." She snapped her fingers in front of him, sending a sliver of carrot flying in his face. "Wake up!"

With a yelp, Noah picked up the largest tray he could find and began loading it with plate after plate. Just what he needed, a five-table backup when Meg was there.

"Here you are," Noah said hurriedly, bringing a loaf of bread and a crock of butter to table nine.

The two couples sitting there exchanged glances.

"We're waiting for our desserts," said one of the men.

"*Waiting* is the operative word," said the woman next to him. She glanced over in Meg's direction. "Must be someone awfully important over there."

Noah blushed furiously. "I'll be right back with your pie and cappuccinos."

They nodded. Noah ran back to the kitchen, making sure to cut extra big helpings of apple pie. He brought them out, then flipped through his order pad and visited each of his tables, asking if they needed anything and taking orders from new customers.

His watch said 8:02 before he had a chance to check on Meg. That darn buccaneer had blocked his view.

To his dismay, the busboy had already begun clearing the table. "Where'd they go?" Noah practically yelled.

The busboy shrugged. "No idea, man. Left their money on the table, along with that." He pointed to a small, dog-eared photograph.

Barely glancing at the money, Noah picked up the photo. It was a picture of him and Meg at about age seven or eight. They were standing next to a bucket of freshly caught crabs on the old pier.

"No, don't touch that," Noah cried, snatching a napkin from the busboy's hands.

The busboy walked away, shaking his head. "Whatever."

Scrawled on the napkin in black ink was Meg's messy script. *I'm on the deck. Don't keep me waiting. Meg.*

202

Just then Tara walked by, carrying a pitcher of ice water. "Good tip?" she asked.

Noah shoved the money in his pocket without bothering to count it. "Great one. Listen, Tara, could you cover for me? Meg's outside, and I have to—"

She plucked his order pad out of his hands. "It's about time. Go on, will you?"

"Thanks a lot." Noah tore off his server's apron and ran outside.

A few people were sipping drinks at the outdoor bar and eating at the deck tables, enjoying the live jazz trio that was set up on the far corner.

There, leaning against the railing, was Meg, her dress ruffled by the breeze coming in from the ocean.

Noah ran across the deck, throwing his arms around her and burying his head in her hair. "I've been so stupid," he murmured, breathing in the clean smell of her hair and skin before pulling away and staring into her face. "I love you," he blurted out.

Her beautiful face filled with emotion. "I love you too."

"I wanted to tell you yesterday, but everything came out wrong, and—," Noah started.

She placed her finger against his lips, shushing him. "I know."

"Did Daphne tell you what I said?" Noah asked, caressing her cheek.

Meg laughed. "Only twenty times. She

wouldn't leave my room until I agreed to come here with her for dinner."

Noah laughed too, his fingers stroking her arms. "You're not sorry you did, are you?"

"No," she said, staring into his eyes. "After yesterday, I couldn't wait to see you again . . . but I needed to make sure you felt the same way—that you weren't just using me in an attempt to lick your wounds from Tara."

"Tara means nothing to me. She never did. I know that now for sure." Noah brought her close. "She's not the girl I fell in love with." He smoothed back Meg's hair. "You are."

"Oh, Noah," Meg whispered, bringing her lips to his.

Noah felt as if his heart could explode, he was so happy. As his lips melted together with Meg's, a thousand emotions flooded through him. Tenderness. Relief. Passion.

And most of all, love.

When they broke apart, he held the old photograph up to the moonlight. "That was sweet of you to dig this up."

"I didn't have to look too far. I've had it in a frame in my drawer for the past year."

Noah smiled, drinking her in. "I love you, Meg Williams."

She giggled. "You already told me."

"And I'm going to keep telling you for the rest of the summer."

Meg touched the edge of the picture. "Do you

204

think these two would mind if our friendship turned into something more?" she asked, resting her head on his shoulder.

"No way," Noah answered, holding her tight. "They'd just wonder what took us so long to figure it out in the first place."

ARE YOU FALLING FOR YOUR FRIEND?

He knows you inside and out. He's the first one you tell when your world comes crashing down around you, or when you have the best news *ever*. So doesn't it make sense that the guy who's always been your best bud could be your soul mate too? Sometimes friendship turns into romance before you even realize it. Take this quiz to see if you're really in love with your friend!

1. Your mom refers to your evening out with your friend as a "date." Your response:
   A. It's not a date! (How could she think that?)
   B. It's not a date! (But I kind of wish it was.)
   C. It's not a date! (At least, I don't think so. . . .)

2. The two of you are hanging out, watching videos as usual. Suddenly his leg brushes up against yours. You:
   A. Barely notice. You're as comfortable with him as you are with your brother.
   B. Move over. It's a little weird.
   C. Blush. There's an electric jolt where his skin touched you.

3. Imagine yourself kissing him. Your thoughts:
   A. Oh! This is strange.
   B. Ewww! What am I doing?
   C. Mmm. What was the question again?

4. He always has a burping contest with himself after drinking a lot of soda, and it used to drive you crazy. When he does it now, it's:

A. Incredibly sexy in a way you just never noticed before.

B. Kind of cute.

C. Still as annoying as ever.

5. When you remember the way you two met, you think:

A. Good thing I found someone I can share everything with.

B. Good timing—I really needed someone then.

C. Good story to tell our grandchildren.

6. You're on a date with another guy, and he goes to kiss you. You close your eyes, pucker up, and picture:

A. This moment, engraved in your heart forever.

B. Your friend.

C. Sharing every detail with your buddy later.

7. He compliments an outfit of yours that you've never liked that much. You:

A. Thank him, then tease him about his bad taste.

B. Thank him, wondering if you were wrong about that skirt after all.

C. Thank God that you happened to wear it around him, then make a point of wearing it again. And again.

8. He's on a date with another girl. This time, you picture:
  A. How happy you will be when he gets back home and calls you.
  B. How happy she makes him, and how happy that makes you.
  C. How happy you would be to see her on a plane headed far, far away.

9. His date was a success, and now you spot him with his new woman, holding hands in the hallway. You wish:
  A. He wasn't holding her hand in front of you. It's just weird.
  B. He wasn't holding her hand. At all.
  C. He was holding your hand.

10. Two weeks later it's all over between them. This information means:
  A. Something, but you're not sure what.
  B. Nothing. You're used to his short relationships.
  C. Everything. The knowledge that he was with another girl was driving you to fits of insane jealousy.

TURN THE PAGE TO FIND OUT YOUR SCORE!

SCORING:

1.	A=1	B=3	C=2
2.	A=1	B=2	C=3
3.	A=2	B=1	C=3
4.	A=3	B=2	C=1
5.	A=2	B=1	C=3
6.	A=1	B=3	C=2
7.	A=1	B=2	C=3
8.	A=2	B=1	C=3
9.	A=1	B=2	C=3
10.	A=2	B=1	C=3

THE VERDICT:

(10–16) There's not much mystery here—you and your friend are just that, friends. There's zero chemistry, and the idea of dating him grosses you out, if it even crosses your mind at all. But that's not a bad thing. He's the one you can turn to when your boyfriend totally breaks your heart, and he'll be there to boost your ego back up and tell you what a babe you are. Good friends are way undervalued, and it's especially rare and special to have a close friend of the opposite sex. So be grateful for what you have and relax, knowing that the comfort level here is at its maximum.

(17–23) You're probably a little confused, right? Your feelings are mixed, or maybe even up in the air completely. You know he means a lot to you, and the thought of him with someone else makes you uncomfortable—at the least. It's time to do some serious soul-searching and figure out where you want things to go from here. Sometimes the most frustrating place for a relationship to be is right on the border, where you two are now. So is he a friend or your true love? Think hard, and don't make a move in the romantic direction unless you're certain that's what you want, because it's pretty hard to go back!

(24–30) There's no doubt about it—you're in deep. The sight of him with another girl makes your blood heat up, and everything he says and does affects you like a tidal wave in a sandbox. So what's next? You can probably guess: You have to figure out if you can go on like this. First, try to throw out some hints and get a clue as to what he feels. If you're still unsure whether the longing is mutual, you might just have to go ahead and lay it on the line. At this point the friendship can't stay the same, because you know you want more. If you come clean about your feelings, you have a good chance of hearing that he shares them. And if he doesn't, you can figure out how to move on from there together and deal with this new twist in the friendship.

Do you ever wonder about falling in love? About members of the opposite sex? Do you need a little friendly advice but have no one to turn to? Well, that's where we come in . . . Jenny and Jake. Send us those questions you're dying to ask, and we'll give you the straight scoop on life and love.

DEAR JAKE

Q: *Josh and I have been dating for a while, and I like him a lot. We have fun together. But he wants this to be a relationship, and I just don't feel ready for that. Can I keep going out with him without having a commitment? If so, how?*

LK, Bay City, MI

A: You said that Josh wants a relationship and you don't. What you didn't say is how much the two of you have discussed the situation. It can be tough to keep going out when you're looking for different things. Josh wants someone he can count on, and you want to have a good time without feeling too responsible. These goals are at opposite ends. However, maybe he'll be willing to do it your way and keep things low-key as long as you agree to think more seriously after a while and make a decision about the future. Making a compromise like that is the only way you'll be able to get around your opposing needs—continuing on the way you are now will be too hard on both of you.

DEAR JENNY

Q: *There's this guy, Roger, who I want to ask out. I like him, and I think he likes me too. The problem is that my friend Marcy used to like him a lot, and even though she told me she's over him and I shouldn't think about her feelings, I still catch her looking at Roger in a strange way. I'm afraid of how she'll react if Roger says yes. What should I do?*

SC, Sioux Falls, SD

A: It's very considerate of you to worry about hurting Marcy, but it sounds as though she's already given you the okay to go for Roger. As long as you've run the situation by her and she hasn't asked you to hold back, you're free to pursue your own happiness. It might be the case that your suspicions are right and Marcy does still harbor some feelings for Roger. But she seems to have come to terms with the fact that nothing is going to happen between them, and so she doesn't want to stand in the way of her friend being happy. It sounds as if you are both excellent friends who care a lot about each other, and I hope you know the value of that, no matter what happens with Roger!

Do you have questions about love? Write to:
Jenny Burgess or Jake Korman
c/o Daniel Weiss Associates
33 West 17th Street
New York, NY 10011

Don't miss any of the books in *Love Stories*
—the romantic series from Bantam Books!

TAKE A KILLER SINGING VOICE, ENOUGH ENERGY TO LIGHT UP A CITY AND PLENTY OF OLD-FASHIONED CHARM, PUT 'EM ALL TOGETHER, AND THE RESULT IS 16-YEAR-OLD BILLY CRAWFORD.

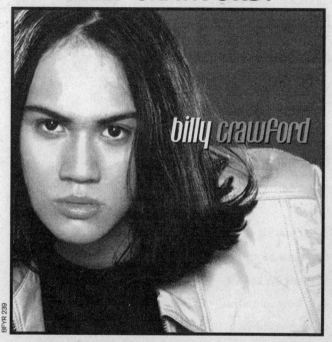

BFYR 239

CHECK OUT BILLY CRAWFORD'S DEBUT ALBUM, IN STORES EARLY SUMMER 1999, AND HIS HIT SINGLE "URGENTLY IN LOVE" IN STORES NOW.

FOR MORE INFO ON BILLY CONTACT HIS FAN CLUB AT:
BILLY CRAWFORD FAN CLUB, PO BOX 884448 SAN FRANCISCO, CA 94188
OR, CHECK OUT BILLY'S WEB SITE AT WWW.BILLYCRAWFORD.COM

You'll always remember your first love.

Love Stories

Looking for signs he's ready to fall in love?

Want the guy's point of view?

Then you should check out *Love Stories*. Romantic stories that tell it like it is—why he doesn't call, how to ask him out, when to say good-bye.

Love Stories
Available wherever books are sold.

www.randomhouse.com

Bantam
Doubleday Dell

BFYR 209